FOR INFORMATION RECEIVED

Short Stories

FOR INFORMATION RECEIVED

EDGAR WALLACE

Originally published in 1929.

Published by Wildside Press.

Visit us online at wildsidepress.com.

Contents

INTRODUCTION
Karl Wurf

It's hard to imagine now, but there was a time when the name Edgar Wallace was more than just famous—it was a literary phenomenon. In the 1920s, it was said that **one in every four books sold in England was written by him**. His output was so immense and his popularity so widespread that he became a veritable one-man fiction factory, a household name whose latest thriller was as anticipated as any blockbuster film is today. He was, in short, the undisputed king of the page-turner.

His life was as dramatic as any of his plots. Born in London in 1875, the illegitimate son of an actress, he was adopted by a fishmonger and left school at twelve. He tried his hand at various jobs—a newsboy, a factory worker, a soldier in South Africa—before discovering his true talent as a journalist and war correspondent. This background gave him a unique insight into the grit and grime of life, which he masterfully translated into his fiction.

Wallace's productivity was legendary, bordering on the superhuman. He authored more than **175 novels, 24 plays, and countless short stories and articles**. His secret? A Dictaphone. He would often pace his study for hours, dictating entire novels into the machine, which his secretaries would then transcribe. This method allowed him to pour out stories at a breathtaking pace, creating intricate plots filled with master criminals, clever detectives, and daring heroes seemingly without pausing for breath.

The stories you're about to read are classic Edgar Wallace. They are brisk, inventive, and wonderfully entertaining. He had a gift for creating immediate suspense and populating his world with characters who, while belonging to a bygone era, are driven by timeless motives: greed, love, and survival. He doesn't waste a word; from the first sentence, you are plunged into a world of mystery, intrigue, and thrilling adventure, where a clever twist is always just around the corner.

His fast-paced, plot-driven style was a natural fit for the burgeoning world of cinema. Dozens of his books were adapted into films, both in Britain and famously in Germany, where a series of *krimi* (crime) films based on his work became a cultural sensation. His most enduring link to Hollywood, however, came at the end of his life when he was hired to write the story for a rather ambitious project. He completed a first draft, titled *The Beast*, before his sudden death in 1932. The film was eventually released as **King Kong**.

Though his star has faded since his heyday, Edgar Wallace remains a master of popular fiction. He was an entertainer of the highest order, a storyteller who understood exactly what his audience wanted and delivered it with unparalleled energy and skill. So, settle in and prepare to be swept away. You're in the hands of a pro.

FOR INFORMATION RECEIVED

IN THE DAYS OF his youth, long before he so much as dreamt of millions, Mr. Roy Emmet Grayson had asked a chance-met boy to carry his bag from one railway station to another, offering him, as a reward, a sum so large that, had the boy been blessed with intelligence, might have set him wondering why his benefactor did not hire a cab. And at the end of the journey he had dismissed the lad with a cuff, and might have got away with his conspiracy to defraud but for the intervention of a large-sized policeman.

Grayson made his money that way; in the fortunate absence of policemen at the crucial moments of his high-class larcenies. Seldom did his signature appear in binding documents: it was his boast that his word was his bond, and his favourite saying was, "You can leave it to me. . . . I'll see you right."

Most people believed him, only to discover that, their services ended, his memory failed to function.

Norma Brayle, his niece and secretary, knew him rather well, and gained her knowledge by successive jars, which rather shook her faith in human nature. Once she had protested. . . .

"Listen," said Mr. Grayson, pointing the wet end of his cigar at her, "you've got a good job, haven't you? I keep you, I feed you, I pay you real money. Want to lose it? Want to go back to the girls' hostel and tout work in the City? You don't!"

"No, Mr. Grayson," she said, a little pale at the prospect.

"Well, see nothing, hear nothing, and say nothing. That's what you're paid for. And get that uncle and niece idea out of your head. You're my secretary, and when I die, the only difference it will make to you will be that you'll be short of a salary."

She hated him and was afraid of him—that was before she met Johnny Westall. And she would never have met Johnny but for the fact that Mr. Grayson left her in Paris for a whole week whilst he was in Madrid, fixing his new iron company.

Johnny was wonderful. He was an engineer, a metallurgist, and a dancing partner of supreme merit. He had the most glorious grey-blue eyes and a smile that was altogether adorable. And he was romantically poor, because he was a young engineer with ideas that old engineers were loth to accept.

Mr. Grayson came back from Madrid, flushed with success, for he had manœuvred a concession without binding himself to giving any *quid pro quo*, and that kind of contract was his ideal.

He did not meet Johnny, but Norma spoke about him, timidly and with a grand attempt at indifference.

Mr. Grayson grunted. He was by nature suspicious, and never grudged time or money to prove that his suspicions were justified, but on this occasion he merely said: "Shut up! I've got something else to think about than your dam'd dancing partners," and there the matter ended. A day or so later, when he was lunching at the Embassy, he heard about Johnny Westall as an engineer, and at the moment did not identify him as his secretary's friend.

One morning, many months later, Mr. Roy Grayson finished the dictation of a letter, and said:

"You know that fellow Westall—the engineering fellow?"

"Yes, Mr. Grayson."

"I'm sending him to Russia. Some new platinum deposits have been found in the Urals. We have got the Russian Government's permission. It will be a fine thing for him, if the report is a good one . . ."

She did not ask what would happen if it was bad—good or bad, the result would be very much the same. There was little need for Mr. Grayson to take her into his confidence. In the privacy of her room she found a letter that had come by the morning post.

". . . I wish I could have met him, dear—he seems to be a very decent fellow. The allowance for expenses is good, and his agent (who made the arrangement after he had spoken to Grayson on the 'phone) says that, although Mr. Grayson has fixed no salary, I can depend upon his doing the right thing. This is the biggest chance I have had, and when I come back I know a dear little flat in Knightsbridge that is mine for the asking."

Norma sighed. She was cursed with the instinct for loyalty, or Johnny Westall would know the value of her relative's promise. Yet, there was a chance, in this case. . . .

Johnny had been gone three months, and only one letter had come to her and to her employer . . . there followed an interval of nine weeks' silence.

Mr. Grayson, with American engagements to fulfil, fumed angrily. It never occurred to him that his niece might have heard.

"What the devil he is doing I don't know!" he snarled. "I'm leaving for America on Wednesday, and not a line! This comes of employing a waster who thinks more of his infernal dancing . . . he's in some pretty Moscow dance hall wasting my money . . ."

In reality he did not think this: in his soul was a growing suspicion that maddened him. There were other seekers after platinum in Russia. Men could be bought—his head swum with fury as he contemplated the bare possibility.

Then one morning came a wire from Berlin.

"Arriving Wednesday," and nothing more.

"Arriving Wednesday! And not a word about whether he has found anything!" he raged. "The dog! He knows I am leaving England on Wednesday—"

"He wouldn't willingly miss his bonus," she said, watching him, and he exploded.

"Bonus! Good God! do you imagine that I'm waiting for that! I never promised him a bonus anyway. He's had the experience at my expense, and he'll be lucky to get anything more."

On the Tuesday night, Roy Emmet Grayson left his sitting-room at the Ritz-Carlton Hotel and strolled out to the Embankment to cool off.

"And who the devil are you?" demanded Mr. Grayson, not without annoyance.

The shabby apparition that confronted him, so suddenly that it seemed to have risen from the earth, chuckled. How shabby he was, the night mercifully hid. Grayson saw only a squat figure and the red glow of a burning cigar, but then his eyes were not yet accustomed to the darkness.

"My name," said the other amusedly, "is Caston—P. B. Caston—suggest anything?"

"It suggests printing machines to me," replied the millionaire, "but as I am not a printer—"

The cigar waved gracefully in the protesting hand of the other.

"I am hardly likely to hold you up outside the Ritz-Carlton to sell you a printing press," he said. "Fortunately, it is so dark that you cannot see me, otherwise you would probably hand me over to the police. For I am a most unprepossessing tramp. I have a four days' beard, my shoes are gaping at the toes, and my trousers are held up by a rope belt."

Grayson was interested—so interested that he forgot for the first time the irritation which had possessed him all that day.

"What is it?" he asked briskly. "A hard luck story? You were a schoolfellow of mine at Vermont—you were ruined by speculating in my Iron Syndicate—your wife played hockey with my sister—or is it a new one you are trying to put over?"

Again the stranger chuckled.

"Wrong!" he said triumphantly. "I've never seen you until today. I don't want to borrow anything, and I've never speculated a penny in any of your wild-cat corporations. I merely offer you my services."

The millionaire smiled in the night.

"Shoot, Felix," he said, for him good-humouredly.

The other pulled at his cigar.

"This afternoon you offered the Western Route Steamship Company a fabulous sum if they would postpone the sailing of the *Carpathania*. The ship leaves for New York tomorrow and you're anxious to cross by her—stop me if I'm wrong—but it is necessary that you should meet one John Westall, who is on his way from Russia and cannot possibly reach London until tomorrow, after the *Carpathania* has sailed."

Grayson listened with growing wonder at this very accurate recital of the situation.

"How do you know this?" he demanded suspiciously.

Again the cigar waved.

"Write me down head of the English Secret Service," said its owner easily; "call me Little Willie Pinkerton, the Boy Sleuth from Baker Street. Read this."

He produced from somewhere a sheet of paper. Mr. Grayson walked to a lamp-post and began reading. It was in Westall's writing and was the first part of a report—the very report on the very property he had been commissioned to make for Grayson.

"Where did you get this?" he demanded. "And where is the rest of it—the report leaves off before . . . before . . ."

"Exactly—before it starts in to report," said the man complacently. "Now the question is, not how I came to get this—I've just returned from Russia—but whether you will pay me for the remainder. One thing I can tell you: this is your chance of getting the first reading of Westall's interesting statement."

"You mean, if I don't buy it from you, he will sell it elsewhere—the swine!"

"Swine or hog or human, it is a matter of indifference to me," said the stranger. "Do you buy?"

"Yes," promptly. "Let me see the remainder."

The tramp chuckled softly.

"Let me see something more substantial than a promise without witnesses," he said. "One thousand pounds net and the report is yours."

Grayson thought quickly. Obviously the report was genuine. He knew the handwriting; the statement began by a recapitulation of the instructions Westall had received before he left . . . but a thousand pounds!

It would be worth that in many ways. The day's start he would get over his competitors, the fact that he would be able to catch his boat.

"I'll give you a cheque—" he began.

"Cheque me no cheques, man," said the tramp. "Cash is the blood of my body. I'll wait for you whilst you get it. . . ."

A queer transaction in the darkness of a wind-swept embankment. . . . Roy Grayson hated to see money go—hated the tramp worse when he counted the notes that the millionaire gave him and found them a hundred short. At last:

"Here is the rest of the report—call a policeman if I have deceived you."

Rapidly the millionaire read . . . half-way through he uttered a cry.

"There isn't any platinum on the property!" he said angrily. "Then why is he trying to sell the report elsewhere."

"He isn't—I never said so. You're right about the platinum; there isn't the colour of it. And with a report like that, I knew (for I have been well informed upon your generous nature) that I might whistle for a bonus."

"*You* knew—who are you?"

"Westall—John Westall."

***

Mr. Grayson did not see his secretary when he got back to his room. He did not even go to her wedding—you can get married on a thousand pounds—or send her a present.

SNARES OF PARIS

I

Johnny Kelly of the Special Branch

JOHNNY KELLY, IN THE outward guise of a gentleman of leisure, stood on the corner of Rue de la Paix and the Boulevard des Italiennes, and he was chewing a toothpick in his contemplative fashion. So he might have stood at the corner of Piccadilly and Shaftesbury Avenue, indicating with a wave of his white-gloved hand this way or that to the bewildered country visitor. For years and years ago he had served his apprenticeship in the uniformed constabulary.

Only now he was in evening dress and apparently wholly dissociated from the police force—though in this respect appearance lied, as any international crook could have testified, for Johnny Kelly, or "J. K." as they called him, was the cleverest inspector of the "Special Branch"—an unobtrusive force which Scotland Yard maintained in all the great capitals. The date was May 1919, and the conditions were ideal for introducing one who more than any other stood perpetually between the snares of Paris and its orders. He strolled a few paces along the deserted pavement—it was after the dinner-hour and the thick stream of traffic moved slowly on the other sidewalk. For here sat those connoisseurs in humanity, the clients of the Café de la Paix. They sat four deep facing the street, and above them the lights glowed and glittered, and the furled red and white sun-blind furnished a suggestion of decoration and festivity.

Johnny had often stood outside the Equitable Building and watched dusk fall over Paris. Mingling with the stars which hung in the dusky sky were millions of green stars and new constellations which spring had brought, for they were budding leaves on the branches of invisible trees, a trick of the arc lights which caught the emerald of the new green and toned the grey branches into the greyer dusk.

Mr. Kelly threw a professional glance along the Boulevard des Italiennes. The Café Americaine was a blob of light. To the left a golden slit marked the entrance to the Olysia, where rough houses might not be expected for hours yet, when the underground café was packed with moist humanity and the "private" dance hall where five franc champagne and women who looked cheaper got going.

He rolled his toothpick to the other corner of his mouth and nodded slightly to an officer of the Surete who approached him.

"Hello, M'sieur Kelly," said that individual, "your man has not turned up yet?"

Johnny shook his head.

"Tigiliki won't come himself," he said; "he's not the kind of fellow who would take a risk—your people are sure that he is up to his old game?"

"Certain," said the other emphatically. "He has a man named Smith working for him. If you can catch him we will put him over the border tonight."

Kelly nodded and resumed his lonesome vigil. It was a night for thought only. Johnny Kelly's thoughts were of a girl. . . . He sighed and eyed the stars again with a little twinge of pain.

In the very corner of the mass which packed the sidewalk before de la Paix, sat two bad men. They sat at a little table under the glass screen, and they talked across their sirops in low tones. They were both men of middle age, grey at the temple, and one was bald. Lex Smith was the notable leader of this pair. To describe them both as bad men is perhaps a little ungenerous to Solomon Levinsky, the second member of the party. He was a pale man with large, white hands. They were large because Nature made them so, they were white because he had been employed in the King's Prison at Portland in "light clerical duties."

Lex Smith regarded his friend with good-natured contempt.

"There never was a good crook with a conscience, Solly," he said; "a crook with a conscience is a bad crook. It don't pay anyway. Look at you. You've been doing five years in an English jug and why—"

"Because I wouldn't double-cross a pal," growled the other shortly; "but that's nothing to do with it, Lex. This kind of job you are putting up to me I don't want, and that's a fact."

"Well, you were in stripes—"

"Arrows," corrected the other grimly; "big, black, broad arrows, Lex."

"Don't make me a liar for the sake of a little error of description," pleaded Lex Smith; "it doesn't matter how you were decorated anyway. You were jailed whilst I was in Switzerland making good money, living in the best hotels, old pal—the Kaiserhof and the Beau Rivage—with wine at every meal, eh? And that's just the kind of life you can have for the next ten years. Now be wise. I've got you to France. I've done everything I can for you, and I need not even take you into this job at all. It's a one-man job and no sharings, but because I like you, Solly—"

"I only knew the girl slightly," interrupted Levinsky, "we had rooms in the same boarding-house—I knew her father."

"So much the better," said Lex Smith; "you will be able to pull some of that soft stuff about the old man—how you used to play Snap together on the dear old farm—"

He looked at his watch—a large golden machine set with flashing stones that glittered in the light of the overhead lamps.

"She will be here in ten minutes, and you have got to make up your mind."

Solly was biting his nails thoughtfully.

"Who is this fellow that wants her?" he asked.

"He's a prince," said Lex Smith enthusiastically. "He's got a flat on the Avenue Victor Hugo that's got Sarah Bernhardt's boudoir looking like a junk-shop. He's got a villa at Beaulieu that you couldn't describe and keep your reputation for veracity."

"And he's black," said Solomon bluntly.

"Not black," protested Lex Smith carefully, "he's lived in a sunny clime, and I guess it has kinder tanned him. His name's Tigiliki, and he calls himself Mr. Tigiliki, though his father was a prince in his native land, which is Ceylon. And he's worth millions of real money, Solly, made it out of tea, and selling his ancestral estates to the hated British planters. He is dark," he confessed, "and he's not what I might call a beauty, but he's got a heart of gold."

Solomon Levinsky shifted uneasily in his chair, and with a jerk of his head summoned a white-aproned waiter. He did not speak till the man returned with the Cognac, and had carefully measured two portions into the empty glasses.

"Give us the real strength of it again," he said.

"I met him in Switzerland," explained Lex, "and that is where I saw her. She was at the Red Cross Headquarters looking after those fool prisoners. Tigiliki saw her one day on the lake and went clean crazy over her, used to send her flowers, candies, and that kind of stuff to her hotel by the car-load."

"And she turned him down?" suggested Levinsky.

"Good and hard," said the cheerful Lex, "say, every morning when the post came, the hotel used to shake. She complained to the Red Cross people, and they passed the word to the British Commissioner or Ambassador, or whatever the guy is, and they put Tigiliki over the frontier into France, having no further use for the same. I came with him. I was sort of attached to him. I saw Molly once, but I knew there was nothing to be gained by persuasion. She is as crazy about a man who was killed in the last attack on Cambrai, and what do you think he was?"

The other shook his head.

"A cop!" said Lex contemptuously, "a low-down copper. Can you beat it!"

"He was killed?"

"Well, as a matter of fact," explained Lex, choosing his words carefully, "he was dead to her. She got a wire saying he was killed, and a printed casualty list. It cost me 250 francs to get the casualty list printed, but the wire was less expensive. Wouldn't you have thought she would have done something desperate? That's where I came in, to advise her, but apparently some old hen in the Red Cross Service supplied all the sympathy she wanted."

"But didn't she write to him?" asked Solomon, "she could find out—"

"There had been a quarrel. She was in Switzerland unknown to the fellow, which I only found out by accident by talking to a girl pal about this affair."

"What do you expect me to do?" asked Levinsky sullenly.

"When she comes you are to have been in the British Army and fought like Hell. You saw Private Johnny Kelly die, and you have some letters in your possession written by him to her. Do you understand?"

Solomon nodded.

"A car will be waiting at the corner of the Rue de la Paix. That looks like it," he nodded his head to a large limousine with bright headlights which was drawn up on the deserted corner opposite. "She will go away with you, and you are to keep her sweet till you reach your destination."

"Where will that be?" asked the other.

"God knows!" said Lex cheerfully, "but it will be somewhere where a Son of Araby hands you a wad of bills, and takes delivery of the goods. You needn't count them because Tigiliki is dead straight where money is concerned. There will be five hundred mille notes, and I shall expect you back at midnight."

Again a pause.

"Fifty-fifty I suppose?"

"Would I offer you any less?" demanded Lex, "here she is!"

He jumped to his feet and his hat flew off.

***

On the corner of Rue de la Paix, Johnny Kelly of the Special Branch was surveying a handsome limousine which had drawn up opposite to him. It was a very nice car, and the driver was a turbanned Hindoo.

"There's trouble coming my way," said Johnny, and he showed his teeth in a wicked smile.

II

What Came of Johnny Kelly

The girl was very pretty. Levinsky could hardly associate this radiant speci-men of womanhood with the lank girl he had known in the old days.

"I remember you, Mr. Levinsky," she smiled, "and I was so glad when Mr. Smith told me that you were in Paris. I only arrived the day before yesterday you know. It was difficult getting away from Switzerland because I had taken on new work," she went on, "but the moment I got Mr. Smith's letter I applied for leave."

She wore some sort of close-fitting dark blue uniform and a wide-brimmed hat which shadowed her face.

"Oh yes, I knew Johnny Kelly," said Solomon awkwardly, "he was in my company. Let me get you some coffee."

She shook her head.

"Thank you, no," she said, "I cannot drink or eat." There were tears in her eyes, and her voice shook, "Johnny and I were—engaged. We quarrelled about a stupid thing, and he resigned from the police—he had a very good position, and joined up. It was really over that we quarrelled. He wrote, but I did not answer him, and then I had a chance to do work in Switzerland for the Red Cross, and I tried to find him, but there were so many regiments in France—and I didn't know the name of it. I heard that he had joined the first British unit which had arrived in France, but somehow I couldn't write, and then, and then—" Her voice shook.

"Terribly sad, terribly sad," said Lex Smith soothingly, "as Mr. Tigiliki said—"

The girl shivered.

"Please don't mention that man, Mr. Smith," she said, "the memory of him is a nightmare. I know he was a friend of yours in Switzerland."

"Not a friend of mine," said Lex Smith hastily, "just a casual acquaintance. A prince in his own country, Miss MacNalty. If I had had any idea that he was annoying you I should have—"

"I am sure you would," she said gratefully, "but you have no idea what I have suffered. He has bombarded me with letters ever since he has been in France, and he is such a dreadful man," she shuddered. "They tell awful stories about him even in Switzerland where the police are so very strict. He has a horrible harem in the South of France, and—"

"Yes, yes, yes," said Mr. Smith soothingly, "a real bad man I believe. I'm sorry I made his acquaintance, but you know when one is travelling, Miss MacNalty, one only gets to know people on the surface. He is immensely rich, and I am told he gives the most wonderful presents to people—"

"Please don't talk about it," said the girl shortly, and turned to the uneasy Solomon. "You were with Johnny—when he died?" she asked quietly.

Solomon cleared his throat.

"I was, indeed," he said, "a grand fellow was Johnny."

She looked from Smith to the other and then:

"Did he leave any letters?"

For a second Solomon hesitated, and his companion kicked him savagely under the table.

"Yes, he left a lot of letters addressed to you," said Solomon, "I have got them out at my house in Neuilly."

"Did you bring them?" she asked.

"Why no," interrupted Mr. Smith, "I wouldn't let him take the risk of carrying them about Paris, besides there are too many of them. Mr. Levinsky thought you would like to go out and take them yourself. His wife and mother will be glad to see you."

Levinsky looked so startled at the discovery of these relations in Paris that, had the girl been watching him, she must have seen through the invention.

Solomon recovered.

"That's right," he said, "they will be really glad to see you, Miss MacNalty. You see I keep the letters in my safe."

The girl looked at him dubiously.

"It's rather late."

"Oh, but they expect you," said Lex Smith with a smile, "Mrs. Levinsky told Solly before he left tonight that he's got to bring you out whatever the hour is. Where did she say she would send the car, Solly?"

Levinsky tried to speak, but failed. He could only nod his head toward the big limousine which was still patiently waiting. Again the girl hesitated. An uneasy sense of danger oppressed her, but she remembered Levinsky as a sober and mysterious personage who occupied the best rooms in the boarding-house where she was staying, and whose business took him out of town a great deal.

And somehow his association with her dead father (Levinsky used to play an occasional game of chess with him in their tiny room) created a faith which overrode her suspicion.

"You have not been in Paris very long then?" said Smith as they rose and made their way between the crowded tables.

"Two days," she replied, and then: "Are you coming out too?" she asked.

"Oh no," said Lex Smith, "I have a very important appointment with a member of the Embassy, but I will see you to your car."

The girl crossed the road a little ahead of them.

"I'll be waiting for you right here on the corner," said Smith in a low voice; "the money's as good as in your pocket."

"I don't like it," growled Solomon in a low tone; "this is an awful business."

"It will be more awful if you come back without that money," said Lex significantly. "Why, what's biting you? The man will treat her fine. You are probably doing her the grandest favour it is possible for a man to do a girl."

Molly was waiting on the sidewalk for them.

"That's your car," said Smith loudly; "good-night, Miss MacNalty."

He took off his hat and grasped her warmly by the hand. Evidently he knew the driver, for they exchanged nods and he opened the door of the big car. The girl had one foot on the step when suddenly she heard a little whistle—a whistle that sent a shiver down her spine.

She looked at the dark figure in the shadow of the Equitable Building, and took a step toward him and stopped.

"I'm silly," she said with a pathetic little laugh, "but it sounded so—"

"I'm afraid you will be late," said Smith; "don't keep Miss MacNalty too long, Solly."

Still she hesitated.

"You will bring me back to my hotel—it is the Hotel Juillet?"

"Don't worry about that, Miss MacNalty," said Smith irritably. "I'll see that—Solly will see that you come back."

"Hotel Juillet in the—what is the name of the street?"

Smith suppressed a curse. He had no idea where the Hotel Juillet was, and to show any haste or inventive power at this moment might breed doubt in the girl's mind. He turned to the man in the shadow.

"Do you know where the Hotel Juillet is?" he asked in French.

Johnny Kelly came forward, still chewing his toothpick.

"The Hotel Juillet?" he said, and took off his hat to scratch his head—a reprehensible practice of his in moments of doubt—and the rays of the arc light fell across his face.

"I know where the Sante Prison is, Smith," he said cheerfully, "I'll relieve you of the responsibility of conducting the young lady to Mr. Tigiliki. Going quietly or do you want me to use violence?"

"I'd rather you didn't," said Smith.

Johnny heard a startled cry and saw in the dim light the girl staring at him as though he were a ghost.

"Johnny!" she cried.

In his surprise he released Smith, who darted across the road.

"Molly!"

She was in his arms, sobbing and shaking from head to foot.

"Molly!" he whispered, and gently disengaged her as a little knot of people came across the Rue de la Paix. In the centre was Mr. Smith, and he was in the hands of a gendarme and a man whom the Special Service man recognised as a private detective.

"Molly," said Johnny Kelly, and his voice was soft, "I'm going to let that detective take you home—I've got to escort Lex Smith to the police station, and I think I heard him say that he did not want any violence."

***

"I've seen a queer thing," said an Englishman who went into the Olysia to join an American officer. "I saw one of your cops beating up two civilians."

"I'll bet they deserved it," said the philosophical officer. "What's yours?"

A BUSINESS TRAINING

It was Winifred Laudermere who suggested the business course. She and Tom and Jarnach were lunching one day to celebrate a successful piece of financing—it was the day Jarnach persuaded their father to put up the money for his motor-car company.

And when the conversation came round to Lambie, Winifred snorted. She always snorted at the mention of the Laudermere "baby," not, as she was at pains to explain, because she was jealous of her half-sister, but because:

"Well, father gets positively senile over that kid. He sends frantic wires to Lausanne, if Lambie's letter doesn't arrive in time for Tuesday's breakfast, and did you hear about his flying—actually flying in a specially chartered aeroplane to Switzerland when she had measles? Flying! and he hates looking out of a third floor window!"

"It must have cost a lot of money," said Tom, with a disapproving frown, "you cannot hire aeroplanes for nothing. I hate to see the old man wasting money."

Any money that rose beyond the reach of Tom Laudermere's rod was wasted. Jarnach suggested as much.

"That's rot," disputed Winifred, "you know father is a fool about the kid. When she comes home from school she'll be unbearable, and so will he. I've written to him—did he say anything about my letter when you saw him this morning, Tom?"

Tom yawned. Lambie was a subject which bored him more readily than any other.

"Yes, he did—said that you had suggested Lambie should take a sort of intensive Business Course—do they take Business Courses at Swiss convents? Tell me, somebody?"

"Of course they do!" said Winifred scornfully, "and—"

"But why this brilliant suggestion, and why this devotion to the interests of Lambie," asked Jarnach curiously.

Winifred raised her pencilled eyebrows and regarded her younger brother with marked patience.

"Lambie must be provided for," she said primly; "anything may happen to father—especially now that he has taken to galivanting around in aeroplanes. Besides if she gets a real business training, she'll be crazy to go into an office, or into politics, or something. We don't want her at home."

The last six words had significant pause and emphasis.

"You sound like one of the ugly sisters disposing of poor Cinderella," said Jarnach lazily. "It is all very enterprising and schemish, and I agree. Not that Lambie wants providing for. She has a heap of money of her own. Mary left her a lot."

"Mary" was their father's second wife.

"I agree anyway," said Tom, nodding at the liqueur whose colour he was admiring at the moment, "we don't want the old man to keep her at home spoiling her and all that sort of thing—here's luck."

Therefore was the intensive business training of "Lambie" Laudermere approved.

There was a very demure, straight-backed girl at the Convent of Maria Theressa at Lausanne. She had a soft voice, a pair of solemn grey eyes, and a certain grave sweetness of manner which endeared her to the good sisters and helped her to a well-deserved popularity amongst the lower fifth.

She had other qualities no less pleasing. One day (some eighteen months after her relatives had sketched her future to their satisfaction) the Reverend Mother sent for "Lambie" Laudermere and Lambie went meekly to the big cool study with its great wisteria framed windows.

The Mother Superior looked up from her desk with a smile at the slim figure with the folded hands.

The Principal of Maria Theressa had once been the wife of a rich Paris banker (you may remember, if you are over forty, the tragic death of the Count Henri d'Avignon and the retirement of his beautiful widow to the cloisters of Avro), and she was a wise woman who had known human love and something of human frailty.

"Sit down, Lambie," she said gently. She used the pet name which Mary Lambton Laudermere had borne since her arrival at the convent. The Superior took a little packet of letters from her desk.

"Do you know these?" she asked.

Lambie flushed pink.

"Yes, Reverend Mother," she said quietly.

Sister Agatha nodded.

"These are letters written by a foolish girl to a man—who is not foolish," she said. "They might have brought great unhappiness to poor Viola Willus and greater unhappiness to her parents. We owe you a debt of gratitude for their recovery."

There was a silence, and Lambie changed her feet uncomfortably.

"I am curious to know," the Mother Superior went on, "how you induced Mr. Sigee—who, I think, is no more than a vulgar blackmailer—to part with these precious letters."

Lambie smiled—a faint, fleeting smile that dawned and vanished in a second.

"I met him in the garden last night," she said after a moment's hesitation, "you know, Reverend Mother, that I begged Viola to come to you, but the poor kid—child, I mean—simply hadn't the nerve. She's been to you since, I see," she nodded toward the letters, "and so I went. He was awfully surprised to see me instead of Viola, but he condescended to discuss things. It was quite innocent—Viola's affair, I mean."

The Superior nodded.

"It was one of those garden wall affairs that you read in—" she stopped, not desiring to admit her acquaintance with forbidden classics.

"In—let us say—Thomas à Kempis," said the Reverend Mother smoothly, "go on, dear."

Again the fleeting smile swifter than ever.

"And Viola wrote the letters and threw them over the wall, and he wanted her to meet him and threatened he would go to you if she did not agree. He gabbled on, such a vain little man, Reverend Mother! I think he is a jockey in one of the Italian stables. I told him how naughty it was of Viola, and what an awful row there would be, but he just prinked and beamed—but perhaps you don't know what I mean, Reverend Mother?"

Sister Agatha smiled.

"Prinking and beaming are two accomplishments with which I am well acquainted. Go on, please."

"So I asked him if he had her letters, and he produced them."

" 'Can I read them?' I asked, and he was awfully pleased with himself and said I might. So I took them and put them into my pocket."

"What happened then?"

Lambie's lips were twitching, and presently she broke into a fit of uncontrollable laughter.

"I'm so sorry, Reverend Mother!" she gasped, drying her eyes, but the Mother Superior was laughing too. Perhaps she had heard an account of this meeting from another source.

"He blustered a little," Lambie went on, "and threatened what he would do to me—so I just binged him and ran!"

"You—?" asked the puzzled Mother Superior.

"I binged him—like this."

Lambie swung her arm round in a circle.

"You hit him?" said the horrified Superior, yet in her horror there was reluctant admiration.

Lambie nodded.

"I just binged him," she said complacently. "It hurt my hand awfully—but I couldn't help doing it; he was such a little wor—, little man, Reverend Mother. I knew he wouldn't follow, and if he did I could beat him for speed—and that's all, Reverend Mother."

The Mother Superior looked at the girl long and steadily.

"I used to be afraid what would happen when you returned home to your people," she said. "Your father I remember as the most gentle soul in the world, but your brothers I am afraid are not . . . but I am being uncharitable, Lambie, and that is the worst of all the sins. At any rate I think you will go back to England not ill-equipped for your struggle."

A troubled look came to the girl's face, but it passed.

"You've been a mother to me, Madame," she said quietly. "I shall go into the world without fear."

"I think you will hold your own, my dear," said the Mother Superior, and stooped to kiss the kneeling girl, "even with your brothers. By the way, do they know that word?"

Lambie on her way to the door turned.

"Which word, Reverend Mother?" she asked.

"Bing," said the Mother Superior, and shook a reproving finger before a face which was anything but reproving.

***

It is possible that the Reverend Mother knew more of the Laudermere family than did Lambie, for there was a time when Paul Laudermere had been attaché at the British Embassy in Paris, and the Comtesse, as she was then, knew everybody, and her knowledge of the family she had gained partly from her own observation and partly from the little pupil whom Paul had sent to her care. She may have learnt something of them from other sources, for the world in which they lived was a very small one. Of the family she could know little that was calculated to strengthen her faith in humanity.

They robbed Paul Laudermere without shame or difficulty. Tom Laudermere, his big, ungainly, elder son, with his monocle and his pointed red beard (pride of his twenty-six years) robbed him openly; Jarnach Laudermere, his second (and younger) son, with less blatancy; Winifred, his elder daughter, married to Sir Colley Garr, was as calm a robber, and had the inestimable advantage of being assisted by Colley, who had lived by his wits all his life.

Each and every one of them had an euphonism for his or her depredations. Tom called his "finance." Jarnach spoke vaguely of "backing." Winifred's was thinly disguised as borrowing, but the result was mainly the same. Father Paul Laudermere, big and hearty, bearded brownly to the third button of his waistcoat, would be approached in the garden, hose in hand, and the end of strenuous tale-telling would be a "Certainly, certainly, my boy" (or "my girl," as the case might be), "You'll find my cheque-book under *The Times*—fill in the amount and leave it for me to sign."

Old Paul (he wasn't so old either) had been married at twenty, had lived seven unhappy years with a lady possessed of a temperament, who had presented him with three children and an accumulation of dressmakers' bills dating back to the days of her girlhood, had prevailed upon him to invest twenty thousand pounds in her brothers' cycle manufactory, nagged him daily for the greater part of those seven years, and had then died.

He married again, choosing a lady who presented him with a baby girl ere she also cried "*Vale!*" to a world which had interested her in the odd moments when she had been free from a gripping pain at her heart.

Thus ended Paul Laudermere's matrimonial ventures.

He superintended, or thought he superintended, the education of his children, cultivated a new variety of pansy, and wrote long letters to *The Times* on the necessity for introducing legislation to check the ravages of bee disease—for he was an enthusiastic apiarist. He had a large house and a considerable estate in Kent between Sevenoaks and Tonbridge, and at one time an income of £20,000 a year in gilt edge five per cent. stocks. He had sold some £30,000 worth of these to invest in Jarnach's motor works at Coventry, had dropped £40,000 in a gigantic deal in cotton (on Tom's earnest assurance that cotton was going sky high), had put out £20,000 on a mortgage of Garr Court, and had loaned Winifred so many thousands that he had ceased to keep account of them.

Paul Laudermere sat in his study, a big pipe between his sound white teeth, a thoughtful look on his face. Before him was a sheet of foolscap covered with figures, a fat passbook, and a neatly-written list of his securities furnished by his bank.

The handle of the study door turned and Mr. Laudermere, in some alarm, scrambled the tell-tale evidence of his perturbation into an open drawer of his desk, and shut it quickly as Tom, his cap on the back of his head, a big cigar in his mouth, and his hands (one recently released from the fag of opening the door) thrust into his baggy breeches pocket.

"Hello, governor!" he said, and looked round the apartment, "all alone?"

"Come in, Tom, boy," said Paul uneasily.

"I wanted to see you," Tom dropped into a big chair wearily, stuck his monocle in his eye, and took a steady survey of his parent, "I'm afraid I'm going to bother you, father."

Paul stared a little pleadingly at his son.

"Going to bother me, Tom—God bless my life, you never bother me. What is it?"

Tom crossed his legs and leant forward. He spoke very soberly, and pointed his argument with emphatic jabs of his cigar.

"You've never heard of Mexican Quarries, have you? It's a company that went into liquidation some years ago. I had a few shares in it."

It was remarkable that Paul had not heard of any company which had gone into liquidation and in which his son hadn't a few shares.

"Now, sir," Tom went on impressively, "we can get this property for £60,000—"

Paul Laudermere winced.

"We need only put up £10,000 and the rest in instalments of ten thousand each, but there will be practically no necessity to put up any more money, because the quarries will show a profit sufficient to pay the other instalments. I wanted you to come to town tomorrow to meet Lord Willus who is the trustee for the debenture holders—"

"Tomorrow?" Paul Laudermere shook his head. "Lambie is coming home tomorrow, Tom—"

A look of infinite weariness came to Tom Laudermere's face.

"Lambie! My dear father! Because a little schoolgirl is coming back from a convent, you're not going to allow a deal like this to fall through? Not that it is necessary that you should see Willus at all—I can fix everything. But apart from that, I wanted you to come to town to see that new car I spoke to you about."

But Paul shook his head, firm on this point. His baby was a very important person. He was unnecessarily in terror lest her half-brothers and sister should discover this, and his attitude toward the shy little schoolgirl who came home for her holidays to Hilltop Manor had been one of gruff and unyielding sternness. This was when other members of the family were present.

"No," he said. "I must be at home to meet Lambie. . . . I want to see her about her affairs. . . . Her dear mother left her a little, you know," he said hurriedly and apologetically.

Tom pursed his lips in thought.

Once before he had opposed his father in the matter of Lambie, and had been shocked by encountering a steely firmness which had not endeared his half-sister to him or, as it happened, to his nearer relatives, since in this matter of Lambie, Tom, Jarnach, and Winifred were one.

"I'll try to fix another day," he said, rising, "but I can take it that you are keen on the scheme—"

"Not keen," murmured his father, "the fact is, my boy, I've had rather an unpleasant letter from my bank manager. . . . I suppose we couldn't realise anything on Torson's?"

"Torson's are in liquidation, father," said Tom irritably. "I thought I explained that to you very fully; it will be a long time before they realise their assets."

"Or those Brebner shares?" suggested Paul in his mild way. "I had hopes of Brebners; you said—"

"Now don't reproach me about Brebners," said Tom, obviously hurt. "We couldn't foresee that they'd lose the government contract."

Mr. Laudermere sighed, and Tom went out of the room, swearing softly.

Down below in the big room which Jarnach had appropriated as a study, the remainder of the family was assembled.

Winifred, a pretty peaky woman, sat on the edge of a table, smoking; Colley, her husband, a florid, young man, was gazing moodily out of the window, and Jarnach, the genius of the family, with his epigrams and his deep turned down collar, was reading with evident amusement a circular which had come by that morning's post. It was an appeal issued by the Breunit Brotherhood demanding amongst other things the supervision of religious orders and the suppression of convents. Jarnach was a "societies" man, and dabbled in church reformation and anti-vivisection movements, but the foaming and intemperate document before him demanding as it did donations to further the work of "destroying the monstrous practices of priest and bigot" left him cold. Moreover, there were more intimate and vital questions calling for his attention at the moment.

Winifred turned to her brother as he came in.

"We've got to wait Lambie's pleasure," he said.

Colley turned from the window.

"What's Lambie got to do with it?" he asked fretfully. He had a hoarse voice and lisped a little. "We can get old Willus to sell for a song, an' there's five thousand at least to split—"

"Shut up about splitting," said Tom roughly. "Any one would think we were burglars to hear you talk."

"Well, ain't we?" asked Sir Colley Garr, with a laugh.

Jarnach made a little face.

"What a coarse beggar you are, Colley," he said. "Tell us some more about dear Lambie, Tom."

"She comes home tomorrow from school."

"Oh," was all that Jarnach could find to say, and allowed the conversation to drift back to money. Presently he interrupted.

"Do any of you people know the Convent of St. Maria Theressa?" he asked.

"Why?" Winifred looked over to him, her delicate eyebrows raised.

"Oh, nothing," said Jarnach carelessly, "only I thought I heard you referring to Lambie just now as a little fool."

"That was me," admitted Winnie, with a slow smile. "Has the Convent of St. Maria Theressa any especial qualities for teaching wisdom to the young?"

"Yes," said Jarnach surprisingly.

He was a good-looking young man, clean-shaven and wholesome, though he wore his hair a thought too long, and he loved creating sensations.

"The Mother Superior of St. Theressa is Sister Agatha," he said profoundly, and ignoring the ironical expressions of surprise, he went on, "Sister Agatha in her secular days was Madame the Comtesse d'Avignon, the young wife of the greatest of French bankers and herself a famous society leader and wit. She took the veil on the death of her husband, and for twenty years has been teaching the young idea."

Tom looked at him curiously.

"Whilst you're in this communicative mood," said he, with a sneer, "perhaps you'll tell us how this affects us—"

"Only this," said the other. "Lady Goreston, whose daughter is at the same convent, tells me that Lambie is a great favourite with the Mother Superior."

"You don't tell me!" said his brother sarcastically.

He got up from his chair.

"I'm going to town," he said. "I've some people coming to dinner tonight. I regret I shall not be here to welcome this paragon."

Neither Winifred nor Colley had any interest in Hilltop other than the interest which Paul Laudermere's views on Mexican Quarries aroused. This was Tuesday, they would re-assemble on the Friday. They went their several ways, and Winifred was in her house in Curzon Street before she realised that she had gone away without saying good-bye to her father.

Jarnach had promised himself the felicity of greeting the child on her return, and went to town with that idea, but spent the afternoon at his club and missed the continental train.

He came down to Hilltop on Friday, travelling down with Winifred and her husband. Tom had motored down.

Had Miss Mary come? She had arrived, said Penter gravely. She was in Mr. Laudermere's study—had been there all the morning.

"He'll spoil that brat," said Winifred. "Tommy, you'd better go up and see father and settle this quarry business."

"Hullo, brother Tom," said Lambie, and gave him her cheek to kiss.

She had grown, he remarked, and was already above his shoulder. She was dressed all in dove grey ("like a convent girl straight out of a musical comedy," he described her).

Her eyes were grey, merging to blue, her hair gold, going brown. She was progressive, even in her features. You saw her growing. Her nose was straight, and her mouth firm above a chin too soft and young to be firm. She was a straight girl in the first beautiful stage of womanhood.

She had a trick of blinking when she was amazed, which, considering she had come right away from school was surprising seldom. But she was Lambie still, with her gentle, apologetic little smile, her soft, soothing voice, her flutters of embarrassment.

"You're getting a big girl," patronised Tom, patting her cheek for the last time in his life.

"Yes, brother Tom," she agreed meekly.

"You must get out of that silly habit of calling me 'Brother Tom,' " he said, "and now you can run away and see Winifred and Jarnach. You'll find 'em downstairs."

She hesitated and looked shyly at her father. Paul Laudermere sat stiffly behind his desk, stroking his beard and frowning with a ferocity which only panic can lend to an easy man.

"I think, brother Tom," said Lambie gently, "I cannot afford the time now. . . . You see I'm daddy's secretary."

"His what?" laughed Tom. They heard his roar of laughter down below and drew an altogether wrong conclusion.

"His secretary. Aren't I, daddy?"

Paul Laudermere nodded and rose with a jerk.

"Lambie is my secretary," he said loudly, defiantly, rapidly, and all but incoherently. "Sound business training. . . . Winifred's idea. . . . Talk things over with her, Tom. . . . Mexican Quarry and all that sort of thing. . . . I've got a headache."

He escaped from the study through the library door.

For a moment Tom stood open-mouthed, staring at the place where his father had sat, then he looked at his half-sister, prim and business-like, yet with a hint of bubbling merriment behind her eyes.

"What the dickens does he mean?" he demanded. "Talk an intricate business like Mex—it's absurd!"

She nibbled the end of a brand new pencil and eyed him thoughtfully.

"Perhaps it isn't, Brother Tom," she suggested humbly. If he had known human nature better, Brother Tom would have been very suspicious of her humility.

She seated herself, with the effrontery of ignorance (so he said afterwards) in her father's chair, and without encouragement went into the question of Mexican Quarries.

"We talked it over yesterday," she said timidly. "You see, Brother Tom, the Mother Superior, who is awfully clever about finance—she has raised the money to rebuild three convents—has given me a lot of advice, I acted as her secretary for quite a long time. Daddy says you want to buy the—what do you call them?—the debentures of Mexican Quarries?"

"My dear little girl," said Tom, in bland irritation, "what is the use of our discussing this? There are certain things one isn't taught at school—"

"Oh yes, one is," she said calmly, "I was taught the principal of good business long before I went to school, the principal, I mean, that should guide me in dealing even with Mexican Quarries."

"And may I ask," demanded the wrathful Tom, "what is that wonderful principal?"

She looked at him for a second—a keen, searching look.

"Thou shalt not steal," she said.

He sprang up from his chair as though he had been shot, his face crimson with passion.

"You . . . you . . .," he spluttered.

"Don't be angry, Brother Tom," she said, and waved him down again. To his amazement, he obeyed her gesture.

"Sixty thousand pounds I think you said," she went on. "Lord Willus, the trustee for the debenture holders, says—I have his wire."

She unlocked a drawer and took out a pink telegraph form and read:

"Have offered property to Laudermere's Syndicate for £4000. Answering your inquiry I cannot honestly say that the property is even worth that."

There was a dead silence.

Tom's face went from crimson to white.

"You see," she went on apologetically, "I know Lord Willus's daughter, and he's by way of being a pal of mine," Tom gasped, "so I wired him. Don't you think, Brother Tom, that the Laudermere Syndicate is asking rather a big profit?"

"Does father know this?" he demanded huskily.

"Not yet," she said softly, "but I've told my own lawyer by 'phone. You see, Brother Tom, I had to have lawyers because dear daddy doesn't seem to have any, and there are so many things that require straightening out. All those funny investments that he has shares in. You know them, don't you?"

***

"Well?"

The Laudermere Syndicate put the question collectively, and Tom answered in two sentences.

He added a comprehensive conspectus of the situation and the family listened.

"I'll see her," said Winifred, and came marching into the study just as Lambie was locking away a big envelope in Paul Laudermere's safe.

"What is this nonsense you have been talking to Tom?" she demanded without preliminary.

"Nonsense, Sister Winifred?" asked Lambie, big-eyed with wonder.

"Don't call me 'Sister Winifred.' Please drop your convent tricks," snapped Winnie. "If you think you're coming to Hilltop to set our father against us—"

Lambie, both hands on the edge of the desk, leant forward.

"I think we will leave your father out of the question," she said briskly, "and we will come right down to a sum of £20,000 in second mortgage on Garr Court—the existence of a first mortgage not having been disclosed."

Here was a thunderbolt for Winifred—all that she had ever dreaded had happened at last.

"I shall . . . speak to father," she whimpered.

"In which case," said Lambie, "I shall jump the whole of the facts into the hands of my lawyers! Now run away and tell Jarnach I want to see him."

What she said to Jarnach no man knows, but he came back to an animated and angry family circle with an air of preoccupation.

"What did she say?"

He shook his head.

"Nothing much," said he.

He walked to his desk and began rummaging amongst his papers.

"I want to find the address of those people who wish to suppress convents," he said good-humouredly. "I should like to send them a subscription. And, by the way," he turned, "whose idea was it to give Lambie a business training?"

Winifred Laudermere might have claimed the honour had she been capable of speech.

MISS PRENTISS TELLS A LIE

IT WAS A STRANGE meeting, the strangest welcome that ever awaited a man from his future wife.

Remember that he had been for two years overseas, that he had acquitted himself splendidly and she, for her part, was as desirable as youth and loveliness could be. He felt the restraint before he walked into the drawing-room, pausing on the threshold with an air of irresolution.

(If the truth be told Jack Wardmaster was not without cause for embarrassment.)

She was lying on her favourite couch drawn up near the window which overlooked the park, and she did not attempt to rise. The air of the drawing-room was heavy with the scent of violets.

He hesitated a moment, then with firm stride crossed to her.

"Hullo, Jack," she said, and put up a white hand, "don't kiss me, old boy, sit down there where I can see you."

He was relieved, yet for some curious reason, irritated. With a little laugh, he sat on a low chair facing her.

"May," he said, "what an abominable smell of violets. I didn't know that violets could be so disagreeable."

She smiled slightly but made no excuse.

"Sorry," she said. "Why, Jack, you are getting better-looking; you're broader and browner. Yes, positively better-looking!"

At this he could do no less than laugh.

"You got my letters?" he said, after an awkward pause.

She nodded slowly.

"Yes, I got your letters. I'm afraid I was rather a pig about writing. You see, Jack, I am so—" she shrugged her shoulders. "I wish I could sell the factory," she said fretfully. "They come here every week and bother me with the accounts."

"They also bother you with large cheques at frequent intervals," smiled Jack, "and, anyway, May, you can't sell it, not under the terms of your father's will. He wanted you to keep your interest in the works, didn't he?"

She nodded. Another awkward pause, during which she twisted her big diamond engagement ring absently. It struck him, by the curiosity with which she was regarding this little bauble that she had put it on that day especially for his benefit.

"May," he said desperately, "I want to talk to you about our marriage."

"Oh no, no, no!" she pulled a little face. "Please don't talk about it, Jack. I know it's hateful of me, but just don't talk about it for a little time. Tell me about France and all that happened there. You won all sorts of decorations, medals, and crosses, and things, didn't you? I saw a picture of you in one of the newspapers—the hero of somewhere or other. I felt quite proud of you."

He smiled again.

"I was always seeing pictures of you," she went on, yawning frankly and undisguisedly, putting her small hand over a smaller mouth. "I saw you in a delicious snapshot, getting out of a car at General Headquarters or somewhere. I remember now, there was an awfully pretty driver, a girl?"

"Oh yes," said Jack, "there was a girl, I remember. As a matter of fact, May, I wanted to see you about our marriage because—"

"Now, you're being tiresome, and I'm awfully worried today, Jack. Won't you come along and dine *tête-à-tête*? Then perhaps we'll talk of marriage and all that sort of thing. Come one night about six; it is my best time."

He rose, a little relieved that the interview was over, a little disappointed that he had not carried his grand resolutions into effect.

"You think I'm a pig," she said again, with a ghost of a smile in her blue eyes. "I'm sorry I am, Jack. Good-bye, dear, you may kiss my hand."

He took the shapely little hand in his and bent over it.

"Good-bye, May, I'll come tomorrow, or perhaps the next day, whichever suits you best."

"Any day suits me," she said, seeming to settle farther back into the cushions. "Push the bell as you go out, I want Annette. And, Jack!"

He paused half-way to the door.

"If you ever see Pitt Sweedon, I wish you'd—no, I won't tell you."

"What is it, May?" he asked, turning to come back.

"I won't tell you," she repeated, "but he is a horrid and an insulting man."

"Has he insulted you?" asked Jack quickly.

"No, no," so entirely with indifference that he was deceived, "I don't know what made me mention him. Good-bye, old boy, come along and see me, won't you?"

He went out, shaking his head.

"Queer," he said. "If this isn't the queerest thing that ever happened and the queerest courtship that ever was, I'm a Dutchman!"

Yet he did not seem unduly depressed, but went off across the Park, taking a short cut to the Cosmos, and had not gone far before he was whistling softly "Madelaine," that song which carried eight million French feet to victory. Also he dismissed Pitt Sweedon from his mind.

It is proverbial that threatened men live long. Pitt Sweedon had reached the age of thirty-nine years, eighteen of which had been prolific in threats, direct, oblique, and anonymous. At the age of thirty-nine he was still a handsome man, not the "beauty boy" who had come down from college in the nineties, but still good to look upon. Many busy years of sowing wild oats had not produced the furrows and pouches which one might have expected on the face of a man for whom life had been a joyous speedway.

The world and its creatures had been his sport. He took where he would, and was wholly indifferent to consequences; mainly the consequence to others, for the consequence to himself brought him no fear. He was a fine powerful man who never shirked a fight in life.

Once in the early nineties there came a blazing man to Pitt Sweedon's apartments intent upon disfiguring him with his two hands. Other men had come with the same intention, but this visitor possessed in addition to a pretty sister (he had left her wailing hysterically in her room) the reputation of a coming middle-weight champion.

The janitor of the flats heard some commotion as he passed the door, and, thinking it was no business of his, walked down the stairs. He and an unconscious prizefighter arrived at the foot of the stairs at about the same time. Pitt Sweedon had dropped his assailant over the banisters.

A wealthy man, a member of a good family, he had a pull beyond his undoubted physical attractions, yet there were men in town to whom Pitt Sweedon was as a leper. They blackballed him from the Old County Club. He picked a quarrel with the chief of the faction which had brought about his humiliation and beat him into a pulp. A week later he was put up again for membership, but in the meantime the wise committee had passed a law, that no person who had been blackballed from a club was eligible for membership. The Cosmos accepted him because it accepted anybody whose name, though it might be without honour, was honoured if it appeared legibly written on the south-east corner of a cheque.

The tantalising thing about the Cosmos was that it was a good club, in the sense that it served its members particularly well, both in regard to food and comfort. And it was in the centre of the pleasure quarter, the only club where a man could dine his women folk and take them on to the theatre without wetting their feet on a rainy night. Therefore, though men might sneer at its quaint membership, and the members might even speak apologetically of themselves, it was successful.

Pitt Sweedon had his friends and admirers who were also his apologists; these talked vaguely about "youth" being "served." There were few members who did not fear him, none, it seemed, prepared to be anything but civil.

Jack Wardmaster, newly back from the war, indifferent to the legend of Pitt Sweedon's frightfulness, if he had heard it, came foul of the man the very day he had interviewed his fiancée. Pitt Sweedon with lazy insolence had taken Wardmaster's homage for granted. It was at night just before dinner. Jack was reading in a corner of the smoking-room when the other had strolled up.

"You're Wardmaster, aren't you?" said Pitt Sweedon. "I've heard about you. You've been doing such wonderful things on the Western Front. I am Pitt Sweedon."

Jack stared up at him, recalling May's words and giving them, for the first time, the importance they deserved.

"I don't seem to remember that I met you in France," he said, and a tinge of pink came to Pitt Sweedon's smooth face.

"I didn't go to France," he said, a little loudly. "I was doing more useful work at home."

"Splendid," said Jack Wardmaster, and dropping his eyes again to his paper seemed oblivious of the other's presence.

That was the beginning of the feud. Wardmaster was worried about other matters, and possibly some hint of Pitt Sweedon's unsavoury reputation had reached him, to add to the uneasiness which May's half-spoken charge had produced. Pitt Sweedon himself should have had enough to occupy his mind. He had received anonymous letters, breathing threats of sudden and terrible vengeance, had identified the writer and smiled, knowing the cause, which was a good one, for the outburst. He never worried about the letters which women wrote to him. He had expected a more serious complication when Tancy came back from Manchuria, because Tancy's wife was notoriously indiscreet and had spasms of remorse and repentance. She was the sort of woman who, in a wild and exalted moment, might tell everything, but apparently she had not, because Tancy had greeted him with his old smile and had begun boring him again with his views on undeveloped oilfields. It was to Tancy a month later that he unburdened his mind and allowed some of his pent-up animosity the expression of words.

"One of these days," he said, between his teeth, "I am going to take that cub and wring his neck."

"Which cub?" asked Tancy, looking at him round-eyed.

"Wardmaster," said Pitt. "If he thinks he is going to make me look fool-ish—"

Tancy smiled.

"Wardmaster's all right," he said. "He's one of the best boys in town. I'm his lawyer, you know."

"You've got a pup for a client," said Pitt. "If you have any influence with him, Tancy, advise him privately not to cross me because I'm a pretty bad man to have as an enemy."

Tancy stretched himself farther back in the deep club chair, chewed at his cigar, and surveyed the lacquered ceiling of the smoke-room thoughtfully.

"I think you take Wardmaster a little too seriously," he said. "He is very young; he is in all sorts of trouble—"

"And don't I know it?" replied Pitt Sweedon triumphantly. "He thinks it is his own private trouble and that nobody else has any knowledge of it."

Tancy was silent.

"He isn't off with his old love before he is on with his new," chuckled Sweedon. "That's the trouble, boy! And I could tell him something—maybe I will one of these days," he added, his eyes narrowing at the thought.

Tancy rose and waved a greeting through the club window to somebody outside.

"My wife is waiting for me," he said. "She promised to call. Otherwise I should sit here and argue with you as to the many virtues of Jack Wardmaster until the cows come home."

Pitt Sweedon shot a quick glance through the window, saw the trim, pretty woman who sat in her car outside, and smiled to himself. He waited until Tancy had left the club, then he took his hat from the *vestaire* and strolled out. It was unfortunate that he came to the turning doors at the same time as Jack Wardmaster, and that Jack, without so much as "by your leave" had pushed in front of him and sent the doors spinning. Pitt Sweedon bit his lip and said nothing. He watched the other as he crossed the road and disappeared from view.

"Some day I'll make you sit up, my friend," he said.

Jack Wardmaster hurried on his way, for he had discovered his watch was three minutes slow, and he had an important engagement which he would not have missed. He came to the rendezvous just as a taxi drove up and a girl jumped out. He hurried forward in time to pay off the cab. Two laughing eyes met his, two little hands caught both of his, and there was in her eyes something which men see only at one period of their lives.

"Let's turn into the park," he said. "I've a lot to tell you."

In the park are deserted walks where two people with confidences to exchange are free from interruption. More important, they are free from observation. She cuddled his arm in both of hers.

"And that's my answer," she said.

"You don't think I'm a—" he hesitated for a word.

"I don't think you're anything but a darling, Jack," she said, "but you have to be something more than a darling; you must go to Miss Prentiss and tell her. Have you seen her since you have been home?"

"Only once," he said, and shivered, and the impression the shiver might convey he hastened to dispel. "She is a sweet girl, Joan," he said earnestly. "It is funny my praising her to you. The whole engagement was wrong, wrong as it could be. You see, we were sort of sweethearts, long before her father made all his money, and we just drifted on, being sweethearts until we were formally engaged. And I think," he said ruefully, "the older we grew the less sweethearts we were. You see, dear, she was so cold and polite and proper, all that a good woman should be, and maybe if I had never met you I should have drifted into matrimony."

"If you had never met me," she repeated, and he caught her by the shoulders and swung her round to face him.

"It was God's blessing I met you, dear," he said. "Probably I should never have known what happiness life held."

"She might—" began the girl, but he shook his head.

"No, no, I'm not speaking against her," he said. "I just hate to talk about her at all because I feel a low-down cad."

"Is she pretty?" asked the girl curiously.

He nodded.

"Very pretty?"

He hesitated.

"Yes," he admitted honestly, and the girl laughed.

"And you are going to give up May Prentiss, heiress to millions and divinely beautiful—I know she is divinely beautiful, so don't contradict me—for plain Joan Smith! Don't you ever realise my name is Smith, Jack; don't you ever wake up in the middle of the night and shudder? Do you ever remember the time when I was a khaki chauffeur and you were a gilded staff officer, and how you gave me tea at Amiens?"

He stooped down and kissed her and suddenly she was curious.

"What are you going to do?" she asked.

"I'm going to May and I'm going to tell her the truth," said Jack soberly. "I must tell her that I do not love her and that our engagement must be broken off."

He thought a moment.

"Somehow I don't think she will mind that much," he said. "I called to see her again the other day; it was in the afternoon, and I caught a glimpse of her on the balcony of her flat as I came through the garden. Her place is on the ground floor, and from the garden one can look right into her drawing-room, and I'll swear that not only did I catch a glimpse of her on the balcony, but I saw her disappearing through the door of the room, yet when I came to the entry to the flat her maid insisted that she was out."

The girl frowned.

"That's strange," she said. "Is she like that?"

Jack hesitated.

"Oh yes, she is rather like that," he admitted. "She goes into the country for weeks quite unexpectedly, and one does not know where she has gone. It was this lack of confidence between May and I which really decided me to end things before I met you," he said.

"Let's talk about something else," said the girl suddenly, and they talked about something else.

He went back to the club later in the afternoon because the club for the time being was his home. His own little place had been let and he was living at an hotel. The Cosmos was central, and here he could reach the people he wanted to meet. One of these greeted him as he entered the vestibule.

"Hullo, Tancy!" said Jack. "You're looking fit and fine."

"I want a talk with you, Jack," said Tancy. "Come along somewhere where we'll be quiet."

"Anything wrong?"

"Nothing—" Tancy hesitated. "Nothing particularly wrong," he said slowly, "only one or two things I would like to discuss with you."

They found an untenanted corner in the Chinese lounge.

"Jack, I want you to be careful of Pitt Sweedon. He's a dangerous man, more dangerous than most people imagine."

Jack Wardmaster grinned.

"Have a cigar, Tancy," he said, offering his case. "I'm a dangerous man myself, if you will excuse the braggadocio."

Tancy looked at the table with the concentrated vision of a crystal reader.

"Have you seen May Prentiss?" he asked.

"I haven't seen May Prentiss," replied Jack drily. "She's a difficult girl to see these days, and I have a mighty urgent reason for wanting to talk to her."

Tancy nodded.

"Queer, May," he said; "a very sweet girl, lots of money and all that sort of thing, but—"

"But what?" said Jack.

"She's eccentric—I don't understand it. By the way, May had a little scene with Pitt. I suppose you heard about that?"

"Scene?" said Jack incredulously. "I can't imagine May having a scene with anybody. Where did this happen?"

"At the Flying Club," responded Tancy. "I was there and saw it. It was just before dinner. We'd been having an afternoon dance. She was sitting by herself when Pitt Sweedon walked over to her and said something. May got up and—"

"And?" repeated Jack.

"She struck him across the mouth," said Tancy.

"Good God!" gasped Jack.

"It was all over in a second. Pitt Sweedon walked away and May went straight out to her car. I haven't seen her since, and—here's the devil himself," said Tancy.

Pitt Sweedon had come into the lounge at that moment, a resplendent creature dressed for dinner and such adventures as the evening held. For a little while he did not see the two men in the corner, but presently he came towards them.

"Hullo, Wardmaster!" he ignored Tancy. "I saw you crossing the park. Have you been to see your lady-love?"

Jack rose slowly.

"See here," said he. "I am not well enough acquainted with you to know whether I am addressing Pitt or Sweedon, or both of you, but to whichever half of you has the brains I would like to say this, that it is not usual to mention a lady's name in a club of this description or any other description."

"You're damned insolent," said Pitt Sweedon.

"And that is just what I'm trying to be, damned insolent," said Jack. "I know nothing about you, except that you're a little indecent, but I repeat you will not mention Miss Prentiss's name in public, or the chastisement you received from her—"

"Oh, she told you, did she?" said Pitt Sweedon, pale and strained. "Then perhaps you would like me to tell you something about the little beast—she—"

Pitt Sweedon was a fighter of no mean quality. Instinctively he guarded the blow to the jaw, but most unexpectedly Jack's right jabbed at his heart and he dropped his hands to guard, but too late. Two smashing blows came like lightning, the second, a terrific drive under the jaw, sent him rolling to the floor. For the first time in his life Pitt Sweedon had been knocked out.

He could not believe it himself as he rose slowly to his feet.

"All right, Wardmaster, you and I will settle this later," he said.

"It can be settled only in this way," said Jack, very white, "that if you mention the name of Miss Prentiss again in a public place, I will kill you."

Tancy watched the two men leave the club, and saw Pitt Sweedon standing irresolutely on the edge of the sidewalk. Dusk was falling, and the park was a place of misty shadows into which Jack Wardmaster melted at a leisurely pace.

Nearly opposite the club, a closed auto had drawn up. Tancy guessed from its shabbiness that it was a hired car, and was wondering who had had the bad luck to draw the poor relation of the garage when he saw the momentary flutter of a white handkerchief at the window of the limousine. It was an urgent flutter and could only be signalling to Pitt Sweedon.

Presently he too saw the summons and crossed the street. He stood for a moment on the kerb by the car's side, spoke to its occupant, and then walked quickly away.

"He's very annoyed," thought Tancy.

Then a woman jumped from the auto, ran after the retreating man, and gripped him by the arm. The casual observer might not have read into the incident any significance beyond the obvious fact that the owner or hirer of the motor-car had remembered something she wanted to say . . . they too melted into the blue spaces of shadow.

"I'm sorry," said Tancy from his heart, and called the waiter to settle his account.

Jack Wardmaster walked at his leisure. He wanted time to cool down for one thing, and only time can neutralise the poison juices of anger; and also he was on his way to another kind of trouble. He had already made his decision to end things with May Prentiss. His task was no less disagreeable after the crudities of Pitt Sweedon. Not that he believed anything that the man had said or hinted. May was not that kind of girl. Nor had he any anxiety to be relieved of the right to champion her or any other woman of his acquaintance. He respected her, placed her very high indeed in his scale of feminine values, only he did not love her. That was a simple fact easily stated—except to the person most interested. Street lights twinkled through the trees before Jack Wardmaster increased his pace. It was a spring evening, unusually warm.

Yet—he halted in sheer amazement.

Park Hall, that very exclusive block of flats, was built almost in the park itself, separated only by ornamental rails and a thick border of lilac and laurel bushes which gave to the ground floor tenants the illusion of privacy.

From where he stood he could see the balcony of her flat, and if that was not the languid May in sky-blue reclining defiant of chills and prosaic colds in the head, he was suffering from hallucinations. A warm evening; but May's chief abomination was any kind of evening air.

He passed quickly through the private wicket and along the narrow gravelled path which followed the length of the building. He turned an angle—it was May. He could hardly believe his eyes, but it was May, in her favourite lounge position, propped with down cushions, her fair hair showing against the blue silk covers.

"Why, May!" said Jack, half-amused, half-worried. "You oughtn't to sit here in that flimsy kit. You'll be ill."

She turned her head at the sound of his voice, and as she did so a church clock boomed out the hour of six.

"Hullo!"

Her voice was cold and distant.

"What do you want?" she emphasised the "you."

"Why . . . I wanted to see you for a few minutes if you could spare me—"

"Oh, go to hell!"

He stepped back as if he had been struck. He was incredulous, shocked, and for a while speechless.

"Go away! Go away!" she wailed. "I don't want to see you, Jack! Don't you understand—I don't want to see you—I—just—don't—want—to—see—you!"

He could only gaze at her, finding no words ready to carry the confusion of his thoughts.

"Damn you!" it was May's voice and was half a sob. "Damn you! Go!"

He turned back on his tracks and walked out of the garden, through the wicket gate he had used and across the park. Once he looked back, urged by subconscious causes, when he reached the spot from where he had first seen the flash of her blue dress. But now the balcony was empty. A light had been lit in the drawing-room, and her maid was pulling down the blind.

"Well, if that doesn't beat the band!" said the dazed young man.

He was making for the Cosmos when he remembered a certain disagreeable incident which must inevitably lead him to a meeting with the disciplinary committee of the club and possibly to expulsion.

He lifted his shoulders at the thought and struck out in another direction which would bring him near enough to his hotel.

The brute! What was the foul thing Pitt Sweedon was going to say when Jack's right to the heart had arrested his eloquence? What had he already told May? Jack Wardmaster stopped in his stride at this solution of her strange conduct. He set his teeth and walked on. Pitt Sweedon should tell him, and he would flog the life out of him until he confessed. Then he grinned to himself in the darkness as the humour of the situation was borne in upon him.

He had gone to the girl to break off his engagement, and she had anticipated his errand by sending him to hell—figuratively, if not literally. But that was not the finish he wanted. He had a man's desire to be punished for the offence he had committed, not an offence of which he was guiltless. She might send him to perdition (he had never heard May swear before), but it must be justified.

He reached his hotel at seven o'clock, and the hall porter checked the hour in accordance with telephoned instructions, and waiting only until he had seen Jack safe in the elevator, he took up the instrument and called police headquarters.

Jack was writing a quarter of an hour later when two men walked in without knocking. They were strong-faced men, and there was something so purposeful and business-like in their proceeding that the occupant of the room did not go through the formality of challenging their right to entry without knocking.

"Captain John Wardmaster?" asked one.

"That is my name."

"Get your hat, you're wanted at Headquarters!"

"Headquarters? What do you mean . . . police?"

The man nodded.

"Good God!" gasped John. "Pitt Sweedon! Did I hurt him so badly?"

"You'd better be careful what you are saying, Captain Wardmaster," said the other warningly. "Mr. Pitt Sweedon is dead."

"Dead?"

"Shot dead—his body was found in the park."

Late that night an urgent message brought Tancy to the cells, and Tancy listened in silence.

"According to the police, Pitt Sweedon was shot at six o'clock," he said. "A policeman on duty heard the shots and made his way to the shrubbery from where the sound came. As he started to run he heard a church clock strike six."

"At which hour," smiled Jack, "I was having rather an unhappy interview with May Prentiss. There will be no difficulty about proving an alibi in those circumstances."

"Thank God for that," said Tancy, with such heart-felt emphasis that Jack warmed toward him. "We shall be able to get you out tonight. I'll go over and see Miss Prentiss."

He took with him the detective in charge of the case.

"Captain Wardmaster is only held on suspicion," said the latter. "I'll take the responsibility of loosing him if Miss Prentiss is certain of the hour she saw him."

The flats were in darkness, and it was some time before Tancy could arouse any response to his persistent ringing at the girl's door. Presently her maid appeared in a dressing-gown.

"Miss Prentiss is asleep, and it's as much as my place is worth to wake her," she said.

She recognised Tancy as an occasional visitor.

"This gentleman is a detective," said the lawyer, "and we are here on a matter of life and death. We simply must see Miss Prentiss, even if we wake her ourselves!"

Nevertheless, the girl was unwilling, and it was only when Tancy showed a sign of carrying out his threat that she yielded. She left them standing in the hall and was gone fully ten minutes. Presently they heard a voice raised in anger, and then the girl reappeared, followed by May. The girl looked half asleep, and she was undoubtedly annoyed.

She had flung a wrap over her night clothes, and Tancy, even in his distraction, thought he had never seen a more lovely creature.

"What on earth does this mean?" demanded May angrily. "Mr. Tancy, who is this person?"

"This person, Miss Prentiss, is a detective," said Tancy quietly. "Mr. Wardmaster has been arrested on a very grave charge. Did you see—"

"Wait a moment, Mr. Tancy," interrupted the detective. "Will you tell me this, miss? When did you see Mr. Wardmaster last?"

The girl frowned at him.

"When did I last see him?" she said. "Oh, I don't know. Last week sometime."

"Not since?"

"No. Haven't I said so?"

"Have you seen him today—to-night?"

"No," said May Prentiss readily.

There was an exclamation from the lawyer.

"Think, think, Miss Prentiss! Jack is held on a charge of murder—the murder of Pitt Sweedon—"

"Pitt Sweedon? Dead—murdered?" she whispered huskily, and passed her hand over her eyes. "I'm glad!" she burst forth suddenly. "I hope Jack killed him. I told Jack he had insulted me—"

"For God's sake, think what you're saying!" wailed Tancy. "Every word you utter incriminates Jack Wardmaster still more deeply! Jack came to see you tonight!"

His voice held a plea—he was begging for the life of one who was more than a friend—he was begging for the life of the murderer.

She shook her head slowly.

"No, Jack did not see me tonight. Poor old Jack, he is a good fellow. I'm glad he is going to marry somebody nice. Pitt Sweedon wrote me about it."

Tancy could only look at her aghast. He knew that Jack had told him the truth.

"He did not come here tonight? Didn't you speak to him from the balcony?"

Again she shook her head.

"No," she said.

Jack Wardmaster spent the first of many nights in a cell.

The day before his trial Tancy came to him. He waited until the door of the cell slammed behind him, then he sat on the hard bench by the prisoner's side.

"Jack," he began, without preliminary, "I've played the lowest trick on you that any blackguard has ever played on a decent man. Wait! Don't interrupt until I'm through. I've let you sit under the shadow of a horrible crime, knowing you to be innocent. I've allowed your name to be dragged through the mud, but always I have hoped and prayed that a miracle would happen and that May Prentiss would come forward and explain why she lied and testify to the fact of your interview. She could have proved an alibi and God in heaven knows why she didn't."

Jack's laugh was short and helpless.

"I've been sitting here for the greater part of a month, wondering just what May has against me," he said, "but I just don't understand what you mean by the other things you have said, Tancy. This case is getting a little on your nerves, I think. I'm glad that you believe I am innocent. That is a comfort anyway, but—"

"I know you are innocent," interrupted Tancy. "I am certain because I know who murdered Pitt Sweedon."

"You—know!"

Tancy nodded.

"Pitt Sweedon was shot dead by my wife," he said calmly. "I know, because I was a witness to the crime, and dragged her through the laurels when I saw the policeman running."

"But—!"

"She shot him because—well, for a good and sufficient reason. Had I known all I know now, I should have spared her the trouble, for I should have killed him myself. My wife left the country by the first Cunarder that sailed after the shooting. She is now safe. But for the quarrel you had with Pitt Sweedon, and your having been in the park at the time, the crime would have passed into the category of undiscovered mysteries. As it is, I have kept you on the stretch—until she was safe. To-day you will be free—I am going—I am going . . .!"

He swayed and stumbled. Jack caught the limp figure in his arms and shouted for the warder.

"Paralysis," said the jail doctor who made a brief examination. "This is tough on poor Wardmaster. His trial comes on tomorrow, and Tancy had the case at his finger-tips. Somebody had better tell Wardmaster."

The prisoner sitting, his head between his hands, heard the news with indifference. Tragedy on tragedy, climax on climax had first bewildered, then stupified him. He saw poor Tancy's substitute, discussed apathetically such particulars of the case as he had already gone over a hundred times, and answered the same old maddening questions.

Some one else had heard of the new tragedy and guessed what it meant to the prisoner.

Joan Smith, sometime chauffeuse to General Headquarters, read of the stroke which crumbled poor Silvester Tancy, and sensed a deeper catastrophe than the newspapers had revealed. Two interviews with her lover, and many long talks with an absent-minded lawyer, whose thoughts were everlasting elsewhere, had given her a knowledge of the case equal, save in one respect, to Tancy's.

She had now twenty-four hours to put that knowledge to good account. Hitherto she had stood aside watching the professional men at work, somewhat overawed by their apparent prescience. Now with all to lose she lost what reverence she had, called straightaway upon the chief of the detective agency which the lawyer had engaged to help him, and found that great man a very commonplace individual, rather stupid and a thought pompous.

"We've done our best, Miss Smith," he began, "I've had my best men trailing Miss Prentiss."

"And discovered that she gets up at eleven and goes to bed at midnight, so far as I can see," said Joan shortly. "Have you found anything which is going to help Mr. Wardmaster tomorrow?"

The chief shrugged his shoulders and shut his eyes, thereby indicating that sleuthdom had exhausted all the possibilities of the case.

"Very good," said the girl, and gathered up her handbag and gloves. "I will see what I can discover. Where did this Miss Prentiss get her money?" she demanded suddenly.

"Why, I thought everybody knew—" he began.

"Mark me down as one who doesn't," she said.

"Inherited," the chief was gruff and irritated. "Inherited from her father, Joe Prentiss. Everybody has heard of the Prentiss Machine Company."

She pressed her questions and learnt something of the late Joe Prentiss.

That morning May Prentiss was not in her best mood. She had risen late and was walking her drawing-room *en déshabillé* when the faithful Annette had arrived with a card which bore a scribbled name.

"Joan Smith?" frowned Miss Prentiss. "Who is Joan Smith?"

"A young lady, Madame."

"Tell her I can't see callers and ask her to explain her business to you."

"I'll save everybody a lot of trouble," said Joan Smith from the doorway.

She was peeling her gloves as though she had come to stay, and Miss Prentiss went red.

"Will you please explain this?" she demanded.

"Yes—I agree that some explanation is necessary," said the girl, who had walked slowly into the room, "and I am going to ask you for an explanation—after you have sent your servant away."

"I shall do nothing of the sort," cried May hotly, "and if you do not go at once, I shall send for a policeman and have you removed."

"Send for your policeman," Joan Smith seated herself without invitation. "Send for somebody engaged in the Pitt Sweedon case. He will be interested."

May shuddered and swayed for a second.

"Come back when I ring," she ordered, but the dark-browed Annette stood.

"Madame, I would rather wait," she said, and for a French maid she spoke excellent English. She turned to Joan. "It is for Mr. Wardmaster you come, that poor young man?"

Joan sensed an ally in this inconsiderable servant and nodded.

"It is better that I wait," said the woman decidedly, "and, Madame, it is better for you to speak truly, for I will have not the life of a young man on my conscience—"

"Annette! How dare ..."

May Prentiss dissolved into helpless tears....

She was the first witness called for the defence, and stepped to the stand, bright-eyed and cheerful.

Jack Wardmaster could only sit in dumb amazement at her cheery smile and at the gay wave of her hand as she passed. Smiling, she nodded to the judge and faced the examining attorney. Given a lead from the lawyer she needed no prompting.

"I knew Pitt Sweedon," she said, nodding. "Oh, yes, I knew him! And if you ask me whether I am glad he is dead, why I tell you that I am! Jack Wardmaster said he came over to see me and that he was talking to me when the murder was committed. Annette saw him and heard the clock strike."

"And why," asked the counsel, "did you persist in telling the police that he was not with you at that hour?"

"Because I didn't recollect," said the girl.

"You didn't recollect?" the judge swung round in his chair.

She shook her head.

"No," she said almost cheerfully. "I was drunk. I am drunk now. Does that make any difference, because Annette will come and tell you? I have been drinking since I was a girl. My father died in an inebriate's home. I had been drinking when Jack came to see me. I was afraid he would smell the liquor and emptied a whole bottle of violet perfume on the carpet. Pitt Sweedon knew I drank. He was rude to me once and I—I smacked his face. I was drunk when Jack called that night. I didn't know he had been until after the detectives had left and Annette told me, and then I just didn't worry. Annette worried terribly," she nodded her head wisely, the mechanical gaiety of her smile unabated. "Annette said she would come to the court and tell the truth if I didn't, but maybe she would not have betrayed me if this young person," she stared round the court seeking Joan, and presently recognised her with a flourish of her tiny white hands, "if this young person had not intruded into my drawing-room. I think the way people come into your drawing-room," she addressed the judge with sudden gravity, "without being invited. . . ."

It took six months to get trustees appointed to her estate, and twelve months' treatment in a private home before anything like a cure was effected, by which time Jack Wardmaster had gone over to the great majority—he had married a girl named Smith!

A PRIESTESS OF OSIRIS

BETWEEN CAMDEN TOWN AND the Gates of Damascus is a gulf which may not be stated in terms of geographical miles. The East and the West are largely incompatibles. The commonplace of either cannot meet and produce by their admixture a third commonplace, as this story proves, if proof is needed.

El Durr, the Carpenter, said his prayers hurriedly—this being the hour of Asr—and finished as soon as was decent, glancing, as was the custom, to right and to left with quick jerks of his head, a reverence due to the two invisible angels who stand at a man's side, marking off his pious performances.

El Durr, some men said, was of the heretical Melawitch, who live up against Beth-Labon—others that he was an Ismailian. This much all knew, that he was a pock-marked young man, who was master of a carpenter's shop in El Kuds, that he was a traveller, and that he invariably bolted his prayers at an enormous rate. Now he came out of the Mosque of Sidna Omar, looking across the Murista a little fearfully, as though he were apprehensive of meeting some one, shuffled hastily across the broad space and went quickly down the Street of Dabbaghin as one pursued.

In course of time, and by a circuitous route, he came to the Gate of Sion, and, halting irresolutely before the forbidding door of a large house by the gate, he passed through, crossed a courtyard, and, coming to another door, he knocked.

"Min?" asked a voice sharply.

"It is I, Durr," he answered, and was bidden to enter.

He waited the conventional minute to allow the women to withdraw, if so be they were in the Mandira, then he went in.

The great reception-room, divaned on three sides, was empty save for the tall man who rose and came to meet him.

"Peace on this house," said El Durr.

"And upon you peace," responded the tall man.

He was young, clean-shaven, and unusually fair. His face had all the quality of the æsthetic, his eyes were grey, and under the plain red tarboosh, the hair, close-clipped, was brown.

This was he who was called Yisma Effendi—to be vulgarly translated "Sir Listener"—British by birth and thought, of Arab appearance, and most certainly the confidential spy of the six nations in the days before war made mudheads of some, gold sacks of others, and of one in particular, a dunghill where a foolish cock crowed a victory which was not entirely his own.

"Take it," said the carpenter, and with his two hands laid on the waiting palm of the other a fold of thin paper.

Yisma read quickly and nodded.

"Who saw you take this at the Mosque?" he asked.

"None, Yisma," said the man eagerly, "for I knelt close to the young man praying, and presently, as I prostrated at 'the merciful,' he pushed this along the floor."

Yisma paced the apartment in thought.

"Tewfik Effendi—is he within the city?" he asked.

Durr spat on the ground.

"May he roast in hell for a policeman," he said, "but he is not. This morning I saw him go out of the Jaffa Gate and take the road to Bethlehem—now I say to you, Effendi, that here in Jerusalem there is no man more fit to die than he, for he is an oppressor of the poor and a taker of bribes—I know a certain place near by the tomb of Rachael—"

"Where he buries his money, El Durr," said the other drily. "All men know this in Jerusalem. Yet none has seen him bury it or take it up again. Now I think you are from Hebron, and they who dwell near Hebron are, by all accounts, great thieves; tell me, brother, why you have not found this treasure?"

The face of Durr twisted in a grin.

"Ashallah!" he said piously. "I am an honest man."

Yisma looked at the note again, a few scrawled words in Arabic, and, despite the mysteriousness of their passage from writer to reader, and for all the furtive passing from hand to hand, wholly unimportant. For it dealt with a certain sordid business at the Armenian Monastery which was remote from the realms of high politics in which Yisma moved. Yet he must speak significantly of Tewfik Effendi, that the dramatic instinct of his servants should be whetted, for his agents worked best under the illusion that, through their activities, the freedom and lives of their fellows were endangered.

Durr lingered on, though he had been dismissed, and his employer did not hurry him. Momentous news came at the tail of such interviews as this. That is the way of the Orient.

"Yisma, you are as a father to those who serve you, and your wisdom is greater than Suliman's. You know that I am a great traveller, and that I was educated in the English fashion by the blessed fathers of St. Francis, and can speak your language and pray correctly in your churches."

Yisma smiled faintly.

"I know that you neglect many religions, Durr. Also that you speak my tongue."

Durr twiddled his bare toes uncomfortably.

"I go by Joppa in three days," he said a little incoherently. "I have a friend who lives in a beautiful house in London; it is in a pretty place called Camden Town, and he makes magic and sees the future and is growing very rich. He has written to me asking that I go to him, for he needs a priest of Osiris."

"Osiris?" said the startled Yisma. "Oh man, is this a new religion?"

"It is a magic of Egypt," said Durr smugly, "in which I am proficient. And, Yisma, El Kuds has nothing for me—it is full of fleas and piastres—and what is a Turkish piastre? I work from sunup to sundown, hewing wood with the sweat of my body, and at the end I have two silver coins to jingle. Let me go, Yisma Effendi."

"Go in peace," said Yisma. "But this remember. It is written that he who serves new Gods must first be immortal. I have a feeling that this will end badly for you, Durr the Carpenter. Go!"

Durr grinned and made his salaam, for he saw nothing that was deadly in Camden Town. He had smelt the cold cities of the north and found them good, and when a man of the hot lands is so perverted that he prefers the drab grubbiness of Camden Town to a cool, flat stone in the shadow of Sidna Omar, his perversion is beyond remedy. So Durr went northward, travelling cheaply—it is possible to go from Jerusalem to the East India Docks for 39s. if you know the ropes.

Bayham Street, Camden Town, is not exactly beautiful, nor was the stuccoed house in which dwelt Ahmed Hafiz, B.A., the finest example of Bayham Street architecture.

Ahmed Hafiz, B.A., was both a teacher and a student. He was a teacher of Oriental languages and a student of the occult. That branch of occultism which he most earnestly studied was the mysterious workings of the feminine mind. He had sent urgently for Durr (they had been acquainted in his early student days, when Durr, a donkey boy of Egypt, had been brought to England by an eccentric philanthropist who had ideas of educating the native) because Durr represented a new source of income.

The reason for the urgency of his call to Jerusalem was Mrs. Sophia Baffleston. Mrs. Baffleston was the widow of a rich builder, and she lived in Torrington Square, and had servants and cats and canaries, window-boxes, and other appurtenances and appendages of the well-to-do. She was rich but cautious. She outraged Ahmed's holiest emotions by beating him down in the matter of fees, and even for the private seances she arranged in her own Victorian drawing-room, she deducted five shillings from the agreed honorarium because the seance had lasted half an hour less than the stipulated time.

He had gazed into crystals and had seen dark men and fair men; he had warned her of a fair woman who was plotting against her (thereby securing the instant dismissal of a perfectly innocent cook), and had emphasised the tender influences of a dark but educated man who secretly adored her; and the net result of his soul's perspiring was (so his books said) the sum of £12, 7s. 6d., which covered the activities of eighteen months.

It was a chance word, spoken at the end of a long, and to Ahmed, boring seance, that put him on the track of easy money. For the first time since their acquaintance, Mrs. Sophia Baffleston betrayed her romantic secret, and Ahmed was instantly alert.

"Osiris, lady? Yes, the great cult still lives. But it is a mystery into which I could not lead you. The priests are few and monies must be paid," he eyed her speculatively, but she did not seem pained. Rather her large face was shining, and in her faded eyes was a light which Ahmed had hoped to see when he had talked of adoring dark men.

"Much money," he said. "I have a friend who is a priest of the Son of Seb, and it may be possible to initiate you . . . even to make you a priestess."

That was it! She was exalted, trembling, bade him stay whilst she brought books that she had read. Rider Haggard's *Cleopatra* was one; she was word perfect, could quote grisly incantations and describe dark and terrible ceremonies. Ahmed went home thinking in thousands, and after considerable cogitation, wrote a letter which he addressed to "Mahmut El Durr, a Carpenter who lives in a small house near the Gate of Damascus, opposite the School of the Jews in El Kuds."

It was a long letter, mainly about Osiris, the Son of Seb, and of Nut, the Giver of Justice in Hell. Mrs. Baffleston had an admirer, who, like her late husband, was in the building trade, but, unlike her late husband, lived everlastingly on the verge of bankruptcy. He was a large, red-faced man with a leer, and his name was Harry Borker. Osiris was a name outside his knowledge. If he had been told Osiris was a giver of judgment in the nether regions, he would have thought it was a fancy name for the Official Receiver. On the day of Ahmed's discovery, he called upon the lady of his choice, and she tolerated him, her mind being so occupied with ecstatic possibilities that he was one with the wallpaper.

"Sophia, don't you think it's about time you gave up this fortune-telling business?" he pleaded. "It makes me jealous to see that skinny-gutted nigger popping in and out as if he owned the place. You're young; in a manner of speaking you're attractive. I always say there's many a good tune played on an old fiddle."

"Oh Set, slayer of my spouse, I am Isis, his beloved, and Horus my son shall slay thee!" murmured Mrs. Baffleston.

"Good God!" said the alarmed Mr. Borker. "What are you talking about, Sophia? I never laid my hands on your old man. And you ain't got a son called Horace!"

Mrs. Baffleston, dimly aware of his presence, pointed a fat and glittering finger to the door.

"To thy hell!" she said dreamily. Mr. Borker went.

In the months that followed, the handsome bank balance of Mrs. Baffleston seemed more and more remote. She was no longer accessible. Every afternoon at two o'clock she left the house, entered her small Panhard (in those days a very classy car), and drove to Bayham Street, where she was invariably met at the door of Ahmed's house by a young man of Eastern origin, whose pock-marked face was one the watchful Mr. Borker grew to know and hate.

Then one day he learnt that his lady-love had given her servants notice, and had placed her house and furniture, her Panhard, broughams, and high-stepping horses in the hands of an auctioneer. The discovery coincided with the arrival of a writ in bankruptcy, which determined Mr. Borker in his plans for the future.

Ahmed Hafiz learnt the news with no less of a shock.

"What is this, Durr?" he asked one day when the novitiate had departed. "What does this old woman intend?"

"I know nothing," said Durr dreamily. "I am a mere slave of Osiris, and She is the Lord's Priestess."

"Stuff and rubbish!" When Ahmed was annoyed, he expressed himself in English. "For three months you have, on your word of honour as a gentleman, promised to get me five hundred pounds from this old she-ox. By Jove! I have only had twenty-two pounds!"

"Have no fear, Ahmed, she will give you riches beyond the dreams of Suliman," soothed El Durr, and would have changed the subject if Ahmed had permitted.

"This jiggery pokery will not do for me!" he said violently. "I have brought you here and given you food and expensive clothes, and now you are going to do dirty work against me! Why is this unprintable woman selling her house? Where does she skip? Ah! That brings chagrin to your face, donkey boy! You are going to take her away! By gad! That's disgusting! After all the trouble I've had with the fat one, and a donkey boy comes and kidnaps her under my very nostrils! Who made you Osiris? Who gave you special speeches and bought incense at nine and six a pack?"

It cost El Durr £85 to appease the just wrath of his patron. He could well afford that sum, for he had hidden in his shirt the greater part of the £500 which an infatuated priestess of Osiris had given him.

Mrs. Baffleston came east as plain Mrs. Baffleston in a P. & O. steamer. None of her fellow-passengers guessed the tremendous mystery behind that plain, stout, and stumpy lady who went ashore at Alexandria. She saw the Nile under the most favourable conditions; the sun was setting and the river was alive with craft. Mrs. Baffleston regarded her domain majestically, and thought she would go on to Thebes by a Cook's excursion that was leaving the following morning, particulars of which she had studied in the quiet of her room at Shepheards.

"Priestess," pleaded El Durr, almost pathetically, "you must not go to Thebes. I have had word from the high priest that you must take your place in El Kuds, where I have a fine house for you."

Durr was thinking of the expense. Contrary to his general expectations, the priestess of Osiris had not handed to him the money she had received from the sale of her house and furniture, even though he had come to her in a state of agitation and ecstasy, and had told her of a vision which he had had, wherein the great god himself, supported by his divine relatives, had instructed her to place her confidence and her bank-roll in the hands of her faithful disciple.

What was more annoying, he did not even know where she kept the money, and although he had conducted a patient and thorough investigation of her baggage, his labours had been profitless. In Jerusalem, populated with his thieving relatives, it would be a fairly simple matter to make the transfer.

Mrs. Baffleston was not mad—no madder than any other enthusiastic sectarian. The dream of her life was realised; she was saturated in the mysticism of a cult which she imperfectly understood; she was swayed by emotions which were both pleasant and comforting; but although her faith in herself had been considerably augmented, her trust in humanity had undergone no perceptible change.

Durr was in a dilemma. The advent of a priest of Osiris into the chaotic welter of religions which distinguish the life of Jerusalem would attract very little notice. The arrival of an English woman, and her appearance in an eastern household, would reach the ears of the authorities. More undesirable, Yisma Effendi, who heard all things, would require an explanation.

One afternoon there arrived by the train from Joppa a veiled woman, to all appearances very much like a score of other veiled women, except that she was unusually stout and short, and wore jewels on her bare hands, which induced daydreams in many a Mussulman's heart. Durr had already taken a house which had the advantage of being fairly remote from the establishment over which Yisma Effendi presided; a coat of blue wash and a few mystic designs transferred a big sitting-room into a temple. And here, for at least a month, she practised mystic rites, burnt incense and joss sticks, invoked Osiris and Isis and extending her fat palms, solemnly blasted and withered her enemies. She had no enemy, but a Camden Town butcher, with whom she had once engaged in a law action. Him she blasted three times a week with great ruthlessness. Durr, pursuing his own mystic studies, discovered that she kept her money in her boots.

One night there was some slight trouble on the Jaffa Road over a question of lamps. As you should know, the Greeks may hang five lamps in the Angels Chapel of the Church of the Sepulchre, four may be burnt by the Armenians and one by the Copts. This question of burning lamps in sacred places is a very strenuous one—did not the Greeks pay 10,000 piastres for the right of burning so much as a single candle over a certain holy stone?—and it became a frenzied *casus belli* on a night in May when the rumour spread that the Copts had received a faculty for adding another lamp to the one authorised.

And there was a free fight which brought out a company of infantry and all Tewfik Effendi's available police.

When order was restored, the police discovered a man lying in the middle of the road, stabbed to the heart. He was evidently a tourist and English, which made the matter more scandalous, for he could not possibly have been interested in the question of lamps.

Tewfik Effendi, a trifle too stout for his office, came to the house near the Gate and had an audience with Yisma Effendi.

"By the prophet I know nothing of this—nor did I see the Nazarene until after we had driven the Copts to their quarters," spluttered the Chief of Police. "Now tell the *Mutesarrif* this, Oh Yisma Effendi, that none of my men drew steel, for we are used to such troubles in Jerusalem." (He called the city "El Kuds," which is the Arabic name and means the Sanctuary.)

Yisma, in his long silk dressing-gown, sat by his desk, examining the blood-stained papers which the Chief of Police had brought. They were business letters, mainly, and a Cook's tourist ticket.

"Did none see this man before the fight?" asked Yisma.

"I saw him," said Tewfik impressively. "He was in the street—this I saw before the light went and before I summoned my police. He was making strange signs to some one at the window of a house."

Yisma saw the body later, a stout, florid Englishman, evidently of the middle classes, not an unusual type. Strangely enough, his clothes had not been searched for money, for in his hip pocket was some £80 in English banknotes.

He had been killed instantaneously by a quick knife-thrust through the heart, and there was still on his face that look of half-amused, half-distressed surprise which is to be found in such cases.

There was nothing to do save to summon the British Consul and the English doctor—and that had already been done.

Yisma went back to his house before daybreak, with no other thought than that a very unfortunate accident had occurred to a too adventurous Englishman who, from curiosity, had sought to investigate a religious riot at first hand.

That night came a wire from London.

"Dead man's full name, Harry Borker, fugitive bankrupt. Remit any assets for benefit of creditors."

"Poor devil," said Yisma. "I wonder what brought him to Jerusalem?"

Yisma Effendi—he had almost forgotten what his name looked like in English—had a network of spies throughout Palestine and even beyond. For in Damascus and Cairo, to name extremes of the geographic pole, were men who looked and listened and told all that they saw and heard into his private ear.

Being, as he was, the faithful servant of several governments, who employed him to watch the beginnings of creeds and maintain a vigilant supervision of all miracles, his time was too fully occupied to worry overmuch about this regrettable incident, which was rather within the province of the British Consul and Tewfik's ragamuffins than his, and although he had given the greater part of a night to his investigations, the matter was put out of his mind when Yosef, his table-man, brought him his breakfast in the morning.

"God give you a happy day," said Yosef conventionally.

"And give you fortune," retorted the polite Yisma.

Yosef set the coffee, fussed around putting plates and knives and fruit in position, breathed on an apple and polished it on his sleeve (Yisma noted the apple carefully—he could never get Yosef out of this habit), and waited, knowing that there was news.

"In the bazaars they say that the Frankish man who was killed near the Bab el Amud sought to ravish the hareem of Bayhum Effendi."

"Who is this Bayhum Effendi?" asked Yisma, to whom the name was new.

"He is a rich merchant who lives here. Some say that he is one man and some another. There is a talk that he is Durr the Carpenter, grown rich."

Yisma smiled.

"Durr is in England serving new gods," he said. "The bazaar talks, to drown talk. In what café does this story run?"

"In all," was the prompt reply. "Bayhum Effendi has a wife who is fairer than snow upon the great hills of Judea. This man came to take her away, and by Bayhum's order he was killed by a man from Gaza named El Khauwan, the deceitful. He has now gone out of the city to his own home, having been well paid. Yisma, he has a twisted nose and is *haj*."

Yisma, who accounted no gossip too light for study, sent a party of horsemen to intercept the deceitful one, and by nightfall he was brought to the little courtyard, where he was informally questioned.

"By my head and my father's grave, I know nothing of this evil story, Yisma," he swore. "I am a poor man who came here to see my own brother who is sick, I and the little donkey I rode."

Yisma considered. To bastinado a man in order to make him confess to a crime which would hang him, is a fairly unprofitable piece of work.

"Take him to Tewfik Effendi," he said at last. "Let him be held until tomorrow."

He sent for the mysterious Bayhum Effendi, but that defender of hareems did not come. Instead, there arrived in his courtyard a flushed and angry lady, who wore the costume of the East, but whose manner and style of talking was distinctly Occidental.

Yisma Effendi sat cross-legged on his divan, for once in his life speechless with astonishment.

"I want to see the British Counsel," she said violently.

"Consul?" murmured Yisma.

"I don't care whether it's counsel or whether it's consul, I've been robbed. £640 in English banknotes! It's lucky I had the rest hidden away or he'd have taken that too!"

"May I ask," said Yisma, "who you are and what you are doing in Jerusalem?"

Mrs. Baffleston jerked up her head defiantly, for she was a woman of property and not used to being questioned.

"I am a priestess of Osiris," she said loudly, "though I don't think there's much in it, because I've been blasting that fellow all the morning, 'is 'ead and 'is 'eart, and by all accounts he's still alive."

Yisma interviewed the Chief of Police, and found that, by the happy-go-lucky methods of Eastern justice, Mrs. Baffleston's evidence was not essential. He went to the station to see her off—an unusual act of condescension on his part.

"No more of this business for me," she said determinedly. "You've got my address, mister?"

Yisma nodded.

"You will send the money by registered post if you get it?"

"I shall get it," said Yisma, concealing a smile.

"I have telegraphed to a friend of mine to meet me in London; I'm going to settle down after this. The things I've had to endure since I've been in Jerusalem! No, I'm going to settle down. Maybe I'll get married." She smirked a little. "Mr. Borker—you've probably heard of him; he's well known in the building trade, Harry Borker."

"I've heard of him," said Yisma soberly.

It was three weeks before they caught El Durr, and most of the money was intact. They brought him to Yisma the day before he came up for judgment.

"For every man, one land and one god," he said. "This man desired the woman's money and followed her to El Kuds, and because I was afraid that he would go to you, I hired a countryman to hit him a little on the head. I think Tewfik Pasha will hang me."

"I think that also," said Yisma Effendi.

El Durr's nose wrinkled.

"It is written," he said philosophically. "Now this is a mystery to me, Yisma Effendi, for if I had stayed in Camden Town I should not have hanged, nor this man have died. It seems to me there is very bad luck in new gods as you said. Let it be known to the good fathers of St. Francis that I died a follower of the prophet."

They hanged El Durr within view of the Mosque of Omar, in the shadow of which he was wont to take his siesta.

THE TIMID ADMIRER

MIRABELLE STOLL READ THE morning paper and yawned. She had read everything, the fashion page, the advertisements of the sales, the ducal wedding, and the serial; and beyond the political news, the Near Eastern war news and the financial crisis (which, of course, were too boring to be more than glanced at), there was nothing more to read. Mrs. Staines-Waltham's house had been burgled, but the only item that really interested her about that tremendous happening was the reproduction of a photograph showing an enormous diamond plaque which was part of the stolen property.

She strolled aimlessly about the grounds, and then:

"Wouldn't it be *wonderful*!" asserted rather than asked Mirabelle Stoll.

She had been feeding the chickens, and had come to Miss Mary's garden by way of Miss Bertha's rosary. The maiden ladies after whom these places had been named had been contemporaries of the big oaken press that stood in the flagged hall of Disaboys Farm, but the names held.

John Stoll looked up lazily over his book, stretched his booted legs farther to the sun, and asked:

"Wouldn't what be wonderful?"

Mirabelle eyed him severely.

"Take your pipe out of your mouth when you speak to a lady."

"You're no lady," said John, going back to his book. "No woman is a lady to her brother."

"You're a vulgar man," said Mirabelle without heat, and in the same tone she would have employed had she told him there was a fly on his nose. "Despite the handicap you mention, I am a lady. And it *would* be wonderful if the New Man introduced romance into our young and dreary lives!"

John Stoll dropped his book with a groan.

"Have you fed those darned chickens, and haven't you something better to do than jaw me?"

Mirabelle wiped a smut from her pink cheek with a forearm bare to the elbow.

"And whilst we are on the subject of vulgarity," said John, reproachful, "ain't you got a handkerchief, Mirabelle?"

"Don't say 'ain't,' and please take an interest in what I am telling you," said the girl, dropping suddenly to the grass beside him. "When I say, 'isn't it wonderful,' you must leap up with a cry and say, 'By heavens, you're right, Mirabelle! It is wonderful!' "

"If you catch me leaping up, or down, or sideways," retorted her brother emphatically, "look round for the bug that has stung me, that's all!"

Mirabelle was small and fair. John Stoll was tall and dark. Her features were faultless; his appeared different according to the angle from which they were viewed. He was mahogany skinned, she so daintily coloured that the village voted her "delicate."

He looked down at her with an amused smile upon his irregular mouth.

"What is wonderful, anyway?" he asked.

"We're going to have a lodger!"

He made a little face.

"A he or a she?"

"A he," she said, and laughed.

"Hence the hilarity," said Jack Stoll, rising heavily. "Well, the cow has to be milked, the hay mown, and the harvest gathered, and the fruit—"

"P'ff!" she cried scornfully. "That means you're going to sleep like a pig all the afternoon!"

"Guessed it first time, lady," said the complacent young man, knocking out the ashes of his pipe.

She laughed and pouted at one and the same time.

"It's bad for your liver—sleeping."

"I was up all night attending the faithful Giles," he said glibly.

"Rubbish! The faithful Giles has nothing more romantic than chilblains—"

"Make that accusation to his face," said Jack Stoll dramatically. "See, he approaches—and with him the Timid Admirer."

Giles, whose real name was Brown, and Eustace Brown at that, was one of those men of nondescript age who are to be met with in agricultural areas. He had the complexion of a child and the chin beard of a patriarch. He walked with that stately, worm-slaying plod which horticulture claims from its devotees, and he was perpetually bare-armed. Winter and summer he was bare-armed. Winter and summer he wore a waistcoat slightly unbuttoned at the waist, and a silver watch-guard attached to a watch, the chief function of which was to tell him when to stop working. The case had been worn thin by what a German with a passion for the omnibus word would call "impatientfrequency."

Following him, at a respectful distance, was the Timid Admirer. The Timid Admirer never walked in front of anybody, even Eustace Brown. He was a little man with a round, frightened face, who invariably carried his hat in his hand, and, from Mirabelle's observation, his heart in his mouth. He lived at the Sussex Arms, the one hostel that the village boasted; and he owned, in an apologetic manner, a Ford car. Mirabelle was sure that, if somebody else asserted his ownership of the car, Mr. Walter Grain would have instantly relinquished his claim.

"Good morning, Grain," said John, and the Timid Admirer bobbed his head awkwardly.

"I thought I would look in," he said a little lamely. "Good morning—good afternoon, Miss Mirabelle. How are the chickens?"

He invariably asked after the chickens; he felt that there he was on safe ground.

"The chickens are splendid," said Mirabelle gravely. "We had a new batch hatched out this morning. Would you like to see them?"

"I should be delighted," said the young man eagerly, and followed her across the orchard to that half-acre which John Stoll invariably referred to as "my poultry farm."

"Well, Giles, where did you find Mr. Grain?"

"Lord bless you, sir, he's been with me all the afternoon. I never saw a more nervous gentleman. The landlord of the Sussex Arms has been going on dreadful about him."

"How do you know what the landlord of the Sussex Arms said?" demanded John sternly.

"I happened to look in there on my way to the village for dinner," said Giles hastily.

"What has he been going on dreadfully about?" asked his employer.

"Well, this young Mr. Grain is that nervous that he went down to the village and bought three bolts and fixed 'em on to the bedroom door. And the landlord says that's aspersion on his character, because nobody that's ever stayed at the Sussex Arms has ever lost more than a gentleman can lose at shove-ha'penny if his luck's out."

"Is he afraid of Nicodemus?" asked John suddenly, a light dawning on him, and "Giles" nodded vigorously.

"That's it, sir. I told him that it was hardly likely that Nicodemus would rob him. He only does the big country houses. And what's this gentleman got to lose? Nothing except an old car that nobody would pay fourpence for!"

The activities of Nicodemus in the county of Sussex were at the moment exercising the attention and destroying the vitality of the local constabulary.

Nicodemus was a burglar with a sense of humour. His idea of fun, however, concerned the police a little less than the fact that he was a very clever cracksman, who, by means of chance-found ladders, and a certain skill of hand and wrist, succeeded in removing the loose jewellery, money, and plate which the inhabitants of Sussex left unguarded.

And as invariably he left, in his indiscretion and good nature, an impudent message, written on the nearest mirror with a handy piece of soap, and that message was usually signed "Nicodemus."

"I think Mr. Grain is worrying himself unnecessarily," said John. "There are plenty of pickings in the neighbourhood for friend Nicodemus. He's not likely to trouble us."

At that very moment, Mr. Grain was explaining his condition of mind to the girl.

"I'm naturally nervous, Miss Mirabelle," he said tremulously. "In fact, I came down to the country to get away from business worries and trouble of all kinds. And the first thing I find when I get here is that a wretched burglar is at large, and I'm liable to be wakened up at any moment of the night to find him—phew!"

He mopped his large forehead vigorously.

"But he's not likely to come to the Sussex Arms, Mr. Grain," said the girl, trying hard not to laugh.

"I don't know, I really don't know. Suppose he did? There's only the landlord, who is an elderly person, and the ostler, who is even older, and me! I was thinking about it this morning, Miss Mirabelle, and I am going to ask you a great favour. In fact, it is so great that I don't know how to ask it."

Did he want to borrow John's gun, she wondered? She was not left long in doubt.

"The landlord of the Sussex Arms told me that in the summer time it is your practice to take in—well, not to put too fine a point upon it, a lodger."

"I'm afraid you're too late, Mr. Grain," said the girl. "We let a room occasionally, but it has been taken for the next month."

His face fell.

"By a lady?"

"No, by a gentleman," she said, "a Mr. Arthur Salisbury. Our agent in Horsham let it."

"I'm sorry to hear that," said the Timid Admirer, "very sorry." Here he brightened up. "But another able-bodied man in the village will do no harm. May I have that flower you dropped, Miss Mirabelle?" he asked.

The Timid Admirer's timid admiration was sometimes a source of amusement, but occasionally an embarrassment to Mirabelle.

"Won't you come up to dinner and meet him?" she said hastily.

Mr. Grain shook his head.

"I should like nothing better, but I'm so afraid of the walk home. It is generally dark, and the road between here and the village is a very lonely one. I hope you won't despise me, Miss Mirabelle, but I am nervous, and there's no use in blinking the fact."

"But if you made an effort—" she said.

"I have made an effort," he said vigorously. "For the last two days I've been making a tremendous effort to—to—say something to you." His voice was husky with emotion.

"Let us go and see the pigs," said Mirabelle promptly.

The lodger came that afternoon; he drove in a fly from the nearest railway station, which was Melbury, and his baggage consisted of one trunk, about the heaviness of which Giles, who had to carry it to his room, complained bitterly.

Mirabelle was in the garden at the other side of the house, and did not hear him arrive, and was unconscious of his presence until his shadow fell across the garden. Looking up, she saw a tall young man, clean-shaven and some-what sinister of face; though she admitted to herself that in some respects he was not ill-looking.

"My name is Salisbury," he said abruptly. "I believe I have lodgings here?"

She got up quickly, in some confusion, and not a little resentful of his attitude. For all the young men lodgers that had come her way had shown marked surprise and gratification at the youth and beauty of their landlady. It was they who were confused; they who declined to see their room, and were sure that it was comfortable without taking the trouble to inspect it; they who murmured their apologies for their intrusion upon a sylvan scene and for disturbing the serenity of its most beautiful adornment; they who expressed their pleasure, in tones of rapture and amazement, at the arcadian loveliness of Little Bempton; and when eventually they were shown their rooms, dissolved into paroxysms of satisfaction, and expressed their regret that they were not staying a year, or even two.

Mr. Salisbury, on the other hand, took both the loveliness of the farm and its presiding deity for granted. He examined the room critically, and immedi-ately asked that the position of the bed be changed.

"I sleep most of the day," he said, "and spend the night looking for glow-worms. I am a naturalist."

"Indeed!" said Mirabelle haughtily. "I am afraid that will be rather upset-ting to our domestic arrangements."

"I only want dinner at night and a cup of tea at about three in the afternoon," said the lodger, and seemed to notice her for the first time, for she saw a light in his eyes which might have been either interest or admiration. She trusted, for his sake, that it was the latter, for Mirabelle despised people who could not see the obvious.

"He's a bug-hunter and he specialises in glow-worms," she reported to John. "He sleeps all day and he roams the countryside all night."

"It looks as though we shall become acquainted," said John sarcastically. "But really, Mirabelle, that is the type of lodger that I have been looking for. If he ever feels lonely and in need of entertainment, all we have to do is to go out and gather a quart of glow-worms and turn 'em loose in his room."

The new lodger dined with them that night—a somewhat silent and restrained meal. Mirabelle was glad when it was over. The conversation was, in the main, topographical. Mr. Salisbury was a stranger in the neighbourhood, he said; and Mirabelle, who knew every road and field path for miles around, was able to give him a great deal of information, which he gratefully admitted might prove invaluable.

Nearer at hand, and under the genial influence of food, he seemed less sinister. He had one disconcerting trick—that of laughing unexpectedly and shortly at some joke which was not wholly apparent to his companions.

"I think he is rather a boor," said Mirabelle when, armed with a butterfly net mounted on a big white cane, he had gone upon his moonlight prowl.

John Stoll was inclined to agree.

She heard her visitor return. She happened to be awake, and, going to the window, looked out. The skies were grey with the coming dawn, and she saw the dark figure against the darker background of the garden as he came stealthily up the path. She could have sworn he carried a bag, though he had taken none out.

He came up the stairs so quietly that she did not hear him, and she thought he must have been unable to open the front door, until a slight noise in the next room, which he occupied, showed her mistake.

The lodger did not put in an appearance until five o'clock in the evening, when they were taking tea in the cool, chintzy drawing-room. He came in, a little weary looking, and, nodding to John, favoured her with a smile.

"How did the worm hunt go?" asked John.

"Splendidly," said Mr. Salisbury, folding a slice of currant bread with care. "I have three or four entirely new specimens."

He did not display the usual enthusiasm of the entomologist and produce the rarities for their inspection, but abruptly changed the conversation, and in this he was helped by the arrival of the Timid Admirer. Mr. Grain was twittering with news which he had received that afternoon from the sergeant of the village police.

"Sir John Bowen's house was burgled last night," he almost squeaked in his agitation. "Nicodemus!"

"Burgled last night!" gasped the girl, and, to his amazement, John saw his sister go pale.

"Yes, last night—or rather, at two o'clock this morning. The butler heard a noise, went down to find the dining-room window had been forced, the butler's safe opened, and Sir John's gold plate stolen—all his racing trophies are gone. The thief must have been disturbed, for he went away in such a hurry that he left a long white cane on the lawn. It is the only clue the police have."

Mirabelle remembered the cane of the butterfly net, and almost swooned.

"Why do you call him Nicodemus?" asked Mr. Salisbury calmly, and John and the Timid Admirer, speaking together, gave him an explanation. As for Mirabelle, she said nothing.

"I had no idea there were burglars in the neighbourhood," said Salisbury, speaking slowly. "Perhaps I have been indiscreet."

He put his hand in his inside pocket and took out a flat leather case and snapped back the lid. The girl's mouth opened in amazement, for, lying upon the blue velvet bed of the case, was a gorgeous plaque of diamonds, the finest piece of jewellery she had ever seen.

"In addition to being a naturalist, I am a jeweller," said Mr. Salisbury, "and I brought this plaque down, intending to make a resetting in my spare time. I think I ought to send this to a bank at once."

The calm audacity of the man took her breath away. It was the piece of jewellery which had been stolen from Mrs. Staines-Waltham, a picture of which had appeared in every illustrated newspaper.

"That is worth at least twelve thousand pounds," said Salisbury thoughtfully, as he replaced the case in his pocket. "It doesn't seem to me to be an intelligent thing to sleep with this under my pillow."

At the first opportunity she made her excuses and went out into the garden. She wanted to think. She must tell John that the mystery of the lodger's midnight ramble was a mystery no longer.

What was the bag he had brought in in the early morning? Acting upon a sudden impulse, she went back to the house, ran up the stairs, and, her heart thumping painfully, tried the door of his room. It was locked. Crouching down, she looked through the keyhole, but could see nothing. Would he go out that night? If he did, it would be easy to make a search of his room.

When she got back to the garden, she found the Timid Admirer, hat in hand, sniffing respectfully at a large cabbage rose.

"I don't like that man," said Mr. Grain daringly.

"You mean Mr. Salisbury?"

He nodded many times.

"There is something queer about him," he said solemnly, "something deuced queer. He has just been saying that he thinks Nicodemus must be a fellow called Jumpy Johnny from Australia. The way he was laughing and carrying on—well, really, Miss Mirabelle, I have a feeling that he sympathises with this terrible burglar. Yes, I do, really! And the idea of his being in the same house as you, Miss Mirabelle, is repugnant to me!"

He glared up at the open lattices of the bedroom, as though he did not altogether free the builder from responsibility.

"He is in the next room to me," said Mirabelle, and pointed tragically.

"Good gracious!" said the Timid Admirer, and looked again. "Do you think it would be a good idea if I slept in the house, Miss Mirabelle? I find I can borrow a gun from the landlord. Or perhaps if I stayed in the garden all night, underneath your window?" He pointed almost romantically to the lodger's room, and Mirabelle did not undeceive him.

She was in a fever of impatience for the lodger to depart. The dinner was an ordeal; and when, instead of going straight to his room, as she had expected, he strolled out on to the tiny lawn to join them at coffee, she groaned.

He seemed in no hurry to take his departure, and was unusually communicative. Watching him, she felt a little pang at the thought of the fate which awaited him. He was undoubtedly good-looking, and she wondered what there was in his face that she could have regarded as sinister.

He was young too, as men go—somewhere about thirty, she guessed. What a waste! She found herself pitying him, and made a resolute effort to eradicate such a weakness. The man was a criminal, a danger to society, and, moreover, had intensified his offence by lodging under her roof.

And then, with a gasp of dismay, she realised what his arrest would mean. She would have to go to court and testify against him, and probably be present when he was sent to penal servitude.

She rose unsteadily, walked away from the little group, and was standing at the garden gate when he appeared, carrying his butterfly net.

"Are you going out, Mr. Salisbury?" she found voice to say.

"Yes, I thought I'd stroll round. I shan't be back till late. The glow-worms do not glow until it is dark."

She gulped down a little sob, and:

"I hope they will not glow at all tonight, Mr. Salisbury—for your sake."

He turned sharply at her words.

"What do you mean?" he asked.

"Nothing—only, I think I know who you are," she said in a low voice. "I feel I ought to warn you of the terrible risks you are running."

He stood in silence, looking down at her, his eyebrows meeting in a frown.

"Thank you," he said at last, and without another word went through the gate.

She watched him till a bend in the road hid him from view. Then she went back to her brother.

"John," she said, "do you know who Mr. Salisbury is?"

"I only know that he's a bug-hunter and a jeweller, which seems to me to be a very curious combination," said John, between puffs at his pipe.

"John, don't be foolish. Mr. Salisbury is Nicodemus!"

John leapt to his feet.

"Nicodemus! You're mad!" he cried. "You mean that he's the burglar?"

She nodded.

"I have known it since this morning. I saw him come back."

John Stoll whistled.

"He was out all night, of course, and Bowen's house was burgled—by gad! I wonder if you're right?"

"We can soon find out," she said. "When he returned this morning he carried what looked like a sack in his hand, and he slept with his room locked all day. John, get a ladder."

"What do you mean?" he gasped.

"I'm going to search his room. I know it is useless trying to get through the door, because it is locked."

"But does he know that you suspect him?"

She nodded.

"I told him a few minutes ago," she said. "When I was standing at the gate and he went out, I warned him. He will not return."

"But—" he began.

"Get the ladder," said Mirabelle quietly, and her obedient brother went at a run, returning in a few minutes with the one ladder which they possessed.

"I will search the room," said Mirabelle firmly. "You hold the ladder, John. Or—go to the gate, and if he comes back let me know."

"I think that would be a fairly wise precaution," said John.

She mounted the ladder and slipped into the room. He had made his own bed and tidied the room, more efficiently than she expected. There was nothing of a suspicious character in sight, and she tried the cupboards. The first yielded nothing, but as she opened the door of the second she stepped back with a gasp.

A potato sack lay on the floor, and, as she dragged it out, it tinkled metallically. She put in a trembling hand and brought out a small gold vase, a racing trophy, and one glance at the inscription revealed the worst.

She walked unsteadily to the window and beckoned John.

"It is here—everything," she said incoherently. "The Bowens' gold plate—oh, John, how dreadful!"

"We'd better send for the police," said John, but she stopped him.

"Wait till the morning," she insisted. "Remember, John, he is our lodger, and he has paid his rent in advance."

"But in the morning he'll be miles away," protested her practical brother.

"That is no business of ours. We must wait until he returns. Of course, he will not return, and the first thing in the morning we will send for the police sergeant and tell him all we know."

She was adamant on this point. Twelve o'clock came, and there was no sign of the lodger. John went to bed, promising to keep awake throughout the night in case of the man's return. Passing his room an hour later, Mirabelle heard his snores, and was not greatly disappointed.

One o'clock, two o'clock came, and although she was satisfied in her mind that the burglar would not return, she lay down, fully dressed, on the bed, as full of good intentions as her brother had been, and in five minutes was asleep.

Suddenly she woke. She looked through the open window for some sign of the dawn, but it was still dark, and, by the little splashes she heard, she knew it was raining. And then she sat up on the bed quickly. Somebody was in the room. She guessed rather than saw the figure by the bedside, and asked:

"Who's there?"

She heard a smothered exclamation, and somebody moved toward the door. With a courage which surprised her, she sprang after him.

"You can't go out. What are you doing in my room?" she demanded, and seized the figure by the collar.

Instantly a hand closed about her throat.

"Shut up!" hissed the voice. "If you make a row, I'll kill you!"

She struggled desperately but unavailingly, and then she felt the hand relax, and her assailant fall back, and, looking round, saw the outline of a head and shoulders against the open window.

"I want you, Jumpy," said a voice, and a beam of light struck into the room from an electric torch.

"Good God!" said Mirabelle profanely.

Standing in the circle of light, and crouching back against the wall, she saw the figure of the Timid Admirer!

***

"In Australia he was known as Jumpy. Nervousness and shyness were always his pose. We didn't know that at Scotland Yard till we got a description through, and then we began to tour Sussex in search of a gentleman with whom timidity was a speciality. And naturally, we hadn't long to search before we found Mr. Grain. I had an idea that he'd go for Bowen's house, and I was watching for him, and just missed taking him. He dropped the swag, and of course I brought it home with me, because I didn't want anybody to know that I was a police officer, though I intimated privately to Sir William Bowen that the property was safe—or would be safe unless some curious individual came stealing through the window—"

"That is very rude," said Mirabelle. "I was doing everything in the interests of justice."

Salisbury laughed softly.

"I think you're wonderful," he said.

"But why did he come into my room?" she asked.

"That puzzled me. I thought he would go to mine because I had thoughtfully shown him a piece of jewellery that was worth stealing. It was a replica of one stolen from another house. He must have mistaken the room."

Mirabelle sighed.

"And now we're going to be without a boarder for the rest of the season."

"I don't think so," said Captain Salisbury of the Criminal Investigation Department. "I've applied for three months' leave of absence, and I really am a naturalist. Are you interested in glow-worms?"

THE JEWEL

"THIS MAN," SAID DANDY Lang, and impressed the point with the damper end of his cigar, "is so rich that he's ill with it, and he's crazy about this wench. When a guy gets crazy on a bird, and he's got that much money, he practically camps in the Rue de la Paix. He never goes to Paris but he doesn't bring her back three years' keep, and he'll fall for this diamond clasp as sure as my name is what you think it is."

He was a tall, dark, not ill-looking man, immaculately dressed. He at any rate looked the part, a well proportioned man-about-town, as he sat under the soft shaded lights in the Arabelle Restaurant. Mr. Hokey Smith, his companion, hardly fitted the clothes or the setting. He was a quiet little man with a ragged moustache and a bulging shirt-front; his cuffs were a little too long, his black waistcoat a little too tight. And gentlemen, as Dandy explained, did not wear black ties when they wore tail coats.

"He's science," said Hokey huskily. "I tell you, Dandy, I'm scared to death of science. Whatever you may say, it's been the ruin of our business. Look at wireless! Once a feller got clear of Southampton on one of them fast packets to America, he was home and dry! Now they pick you up in the middle of the sea and ask the captain the colour of your eyebrows. It looks an easy job, I grant you, but this Macready fellow's science, and once you get going after science you're finished."

His companion looked at him with a calm and only slightly malignant eye.

"The trouble with you, Hokey," he said gently, "is that you're not educated. Macready is not more scientific than you and less than me. He goes in for all kinds of push-the-button gadgets, I admit, but we're not burgling his house. If we were, that would be another story. The minute you stepped on a mat you'd hear the Soldiers' Chorus from *Faust*."

"Who's she?" asked Hokey, who never lost an opportunity of acquiring knowledge.

"And if you walked up the stairs, you'd probably fire six rockets from the roof. But he won't carry any of those contraptions on a railway journey, and it's a million pounds to fourpence that if we don't get him in France we'll get him between Dover and London. He always travels by the midnight sleeper from Paris. Now are you on? We cut two ways, share and share alike. It's an easier job than the emeralds we got from that American woman."

Hokey hesitated, shook his head half-heartedly, sighed again.

"I don't like interfering with science," he said, and, as he saw the lips of his companion curl in a snarl, he added hastily: "I'll take you!"

Mr. John Macready had every reason to pay homage at the shrine of science. For had not a maternal uncle discovered a method of hardening steel, and his own father built up a fortune of fabulous dimensions out of organised electricity?

He was lamenting his own failure that very night when the enemies of society planned his undoing; and he had a sympathetic audience, for the pretty girl who sat beside him on the floor before a big fire in his house in Berkeley Square, and helped herself to cigarettes from his case with that proprietorial air which a woman acquires during the period of her courtship and loses so quickly after marriage, had no doubt at all that John Macready outrivalled his illustrious relations in inventiveness, brilliancy of intellect, and financial genius.

"I don't want to come to you, darling, with nothing but money," he proclaimed fervently. "I want to bring Achievement. I want to Find Something, exploit it, add a pound to every pound I've inherited; and I think I'm on the track of The Very Big."

He was fair and tall, very good-looking, extremely enthusiastic. Her eyes kindled to that enthusiasm.

"I do understand that, darling," she breathed. "It is so perfectly ghastly to hear people say: 'Oh yes, if he hadn't inherited the money he would never have made it.'"

In gratitude and love he swooned towards her, and for twenty-five minutes sane conversation was interrupted.

She came to earth by way of that interesting thoroughfare of Paris which Dandy Lang had mentioned.

". . . It's the most gorgeous plaque you ever saw. Lecomte wants eighteen thousand for it, but I think he'll take less. You simply must have it, beloved. It shall be your wedding present."

"Oh no," she murmured; "darling, it is so extravagant of you!"

She said this in that tone of cooing regret which women employ when they are accepting a present that a man cannot afford.

But John Macready could afford this and more.

"I'll combine business with pleasure," he said. "I've got to go over and see this man Arkwright, and he's going to be a pretty tough proposition. You

know what these Americans are. If I can only get him to my way of thinking.
..."

At this point Mr. John Macready became really scientific, helped his lady love to her feet, and from now on they sat at a table, whilst he illustrated, with pencil and paper, the benefits and joys he hoped to bring to the world, and (in parallel columns) the steady accretion to his already bloated income which would arise as a direct consequence of his philanthropy.

Three days later, Hokey Smith, shivering miserably, his face a pale apple-green, for the crossing had been a rough one, stood beside his more debonair companion and watched Mr. Macready pass rapidly along the rain-soaked platform at Calais and climb into a Pullman. He was travelling alone, as was his custom.

"In you get, Hokey," said Mr. Lang under his breath. "He's aboard."

"Don't say 'aboard,' " said Hokey, with a shudder and added, with a little spirit: "I don't see how he could get to Paris any other way unless he walked."

"He might have gone to Berlin, you poor fish!" said the guiding light of the enterprise. "Ever since that broker got into the wrong train at Calais I've been careful."

Dandy's knowledge of France and of French railways was a very extensive one—not a remarkable fact, since he had "worked" the Continent for the greater part of twelve years, and was the most expert luggage thief in Europe. And he would add complacently to his confidant, "without a conviction."

Paris he knew, French he spoke. To Hokey Smith, all countries and languages were foreign and meaningless.

There were times when Mr. Lang regretted the necessity for bringing his companion; but Hokey was a clever "mover"; it was said that he could take a pillow from under a sleeper's head without occasioning him the least discomfort or causing him to stir in his slumbers. And he was a marvellous duplicator of bags. It was exactly for this quality that he had been chosen.

As a trailer he was valueless; spent most of his time while they were in Paris looking for improper pictures in the French illustrated newspapers, and hardly left his hotel. Dandy, on the other hand, only came in to sleep and report.

"He's been three times to Lecomte, the jeweller, and he's getting the stuff this afternoon," he reported at last. "I went into the shop while he was there, and heard him say: 'I want a very special case for this'; and here's a copy of the wire he sent from his hotel."

He pushed a slip of paper across to Hokey Smith, who adjusted his pince-nez—for he was really a very respectable-looking man—and read:

"Have got the jewel! Leaving Paris tonight. Keep your congratulations until I arrive."

"I've booked sleepers for tonight," said Dandy. "I am depending on you."

Hokey Smith rubbed his bald head and looked disconsolately out into the gloomy streets of Paris—it had not stopped raining since they arrived.

"If there's no science in it, I'll get it," he said. "Do you know what his bag looks like?"

This was an important question. Mr. Smith carried with him a peculiar equipment. He was an expert bagmaker, and, given an hour, could manufacture an exact duplicate of any valise for which he had to find a substitute.

"I'll find out," said Dandy, and the rest of the day he spent in intensive observation.

In a sense Mr. John Macready was a very difficult man to trail. Perhaps "boring" would be a better word, for he spent quite a lot of his time in the company of an American inventor named Arkwright, who was an interminable conversationalist. He had a laboratory out towards Auteuil, and was, as the watcher discovered, something of a figure in the world of applied science. Dandy's observation and espionage, however, was profitable.

He missed Mr. Macready for an hour, but picked him up again outside his hotel, the Bristol, just before seven in the evening. His taxi came from the direction of the Rue de la Paix, and he was accompanied by a man who had the appearance of a French detective. He took from the cab, with the greatest care, an attaché case of red morocco, and this he carried, refusing the porter's offer to relieve him of his burden, into the hotel. Dandy noted the size, shape, and colouring, and saw near the handle an inscription in gold lettering. And then Mr. Macready and his escort disappeared into the vestibule of the Bristol.

He came back quickly to Hokey and gave him the dimensions and appearance of the case.

"He had a French 'busy' with him—if Macready takes the man to London with him, it's good-bye eighteen thousand quid!"

Hokey, who was no fool, though a bad sailor, pulled at his plump chin.

"A shot of morph in a cigarette has been known to work wonders," he said, and added: "And it's scientific. I'll take care of the 'busy.'"

It was a wild night when the train pulled out of the Gare du Nord, and Dandy, looking through the window of the sleeping car, had the infinite satisfaction of seeing the bareheaded French detective left behind on the platform. If the energy and the humility of his parting salutations meant anything, he was the best-tipped detective in Paris that night.

Mr. Hokey Smith had not been entirely idle whilst the train was standing in the station. He came into a sleeping compartment which his friend shared, opened his big bag and put the finishing touches to a small red morocco case that he had been working on with such industry that evening.

"The size is right to the eighth of an inch," he said complacently, "and the lettering is usual."

"Did you get it?" asked Dandy eagerly.

Mr. Smith nodded.

" 'The Jewel,' " he said; and, despairingly: "You wouldn't think that a man of intelligence and science would put a label on a thing like that, would you?"

Whatever doubt they had as to the contents of the attaché case was dispelled when they went into the supper car which was attached to the train. Mr. Macready came in, carrying the red morocco case, which he put between his feet when he sat down to the table. They followed him closely along the narrow corridor back to his sleeping berth. Macready occupied this alone, and presumably paid double fare for the privilege. Between his compartment and that occupied by the two adventurers was a small washplace, and it was possible, supposing he were careless and did not lock the communicating door, to pass from one compartment to the other. Mr. Macready was not careless, and when, in the dead of night, Hokey tried the door, he found it most securely locked.

To force it would not be a difficult matter, but it would make a great deal of noise. It was much easier to enter from the corridor, and after Hokey had gone along to keep guard outside the little compartment where the conductor was dozing, Dandy inserted a key gently, lifted the latch of the door, slid it back gingerly, and stepped inside. As he did so, he drew up a hand kerchief which he had knotted round his neck, so that the lower part of his features was concealed.

He pulled the door close after him, gently unfastened the door communicating with the washplace, as a quick way of escape, and began to make his investigations, with the help of a tiny electric lamp which threw a pinpoint of light. The attaché case was not on the luggage rack or on the spare seat. He heard Macready move and grunt, and switched off the light. Presently came the sound of heavy breathing, and he tried again.

It was not long before he located the red attaché case. It was humped under the bedclothes at the sleeper's feet. Gingerly he inserted his hand, and found a piece of cord firmly knotted to the handle. The other end was possibly fastened round Macready's ankle.

He was feeling for his nippers when somebody rapped at the outer door, and a voice in French demanded:

"Is all well, Monsieur?"

Dandy had only time to slip into the washplace, and softly fasten the catch from the inside, before he heard Mr. Macready's sleepy voice say:

"All right, conductor."

Evidently there was a working arrangement by which the conductor should call him at regular intervals.

When he got to his own compartment he found Hokey already there.

"That French bird had an alarm clock. It buzzed off just after you'd got into the sleeper," he said.

They waited for half an hour, and were preparing to make their second attempt when they heard the bell ring in the corridor, and a few moments afterwards a conversation between Macready and the conductor. Apparently the young man was restless. They heard him ask the conductor to make coffee for him:

"That lets us out," groaned Dandy. "The chance of getting it on the boat is one in a million. That man's got a hell of a conscience, or he'd be able to sleep!"

But luck was not entirely against them. They arrived at Calais in the grey dawn; the wind howled and whistled round the bleak station buildings; the boat lying by the side of the quay pitched and tossed as though it were in mid-Channel rather than in calm harbour waters. There was an announcement on the platform that the boat would not sail owing to the gale raging in the Channel.

For two hours they hung about the station; then they saw Mr. Macready drive off with his precious red case, and followed him. He went to an hotel, engaged a room, with orders that he was to be called at midday. Dandy made a reconnaissance, and returned discouraged.

"This hotel's full of waiters who've got nothing else to do but look after Macready," he said.

At two o'clock that afternoon the storm-tossed *Maid of Kent* wallowed and rolled her way into Dover Harbour. She carried a small complement of passengers who did not care. Hokey Smith was dragged limply to firm land, propped against a wall. By the time he had recovered, Mr. Lang had got his meagre baggage through the Customs. He also carried a small attaché case with a brown canvas cover. This was not remarkable, for he had carried the dummy case since he arrived at Boulogne.

They found a compartment for themselves and the train drew out.

"If ever I take a trip like this again," said Hokey faintly, "you can punch me on the nose and I'll say thank you. All this time wasted . . . and that ship. . . . Oh God!"

"Wasted nothing," said Dandy, and there was a strange look in his eyes.

"What's science doing?" wailed Mr. Smith. "They ought to have had a tunnel years ago—"

"Tunnels are no good to me," said Dandy. "Did you see Macready?" he demanded. "They had to carry him, almost, to the Lord Warden. He's greener than you—and anything greener than you is blue. Look!"

He unsnapped the cover of the attaché case, and Hokey Smith was not so sick that he could not see that the case was not the thing he had made.

"You got it!" he exploded, and Dandy smiled.

"When that fellow was lying in his state-room, waiting and hoping for death, I went inside and made the change. It was easier than biting butter! Let's have a look at a lot of money."

He tried to unfasten the clasps, but they were firmly locked.

"It'll do in London," urged Smith. "If you chuck the case out of the window, it'll only give 'em a clue."

As the train was running into Victoria, Dandy took another look at the red morocco attaché case. In the centre, between the locks, was a small dial which moved in his hand. He thought it was a combination lock, but he had no time to make further investigations. The train came to a standstill, and he stepped on to the crowded platform, carrying the case in his hand. And then:

"*Good evening, everybody! Good evening, Doris May of Camberwell! Many happy returns! If you look under the sofa you'll find a beautiful little present. Hullo, Mary Agnes of Walthamstow! Many happy returns! I'm glad your father has bought you a nice push-cart....*"

Dandy stood paralysed. The voice was coming from the attaché case. Everybody was staring at him.

"*Good evening, Mary Jones of Brixton! If you'll look behind the piano you'll see such a beautiful little thing that Daddy's bought you for a birthday present....*"

Somebody took Dandy Lang by the arm.

"Going quietly?"

Dandy looked round slowly into an inspectorial face, not unfamiliar.

"It's a cop! What's the idea?"

The inspector looked at him reproachfully.

"If you *will* go pinching portable wireless sets, you must expect to get into trouble," he said.

In the cab that carried them to Rochester Row Police Station, Hokey Smith made one comment.

"This comes of messin' about with science," he said.

***

"I missed the case the moment I got to the hotel," John Macready told his bride-to-be, "and I was simply frantic, and wired the police in London. I had given this inventor fellow a bond that the instrument should not pass out of my hands until the patents were in order. It's the loudest-speaking portable that the world has ever known. I called it 'The Jewel,' darling. Oh, by the way," he put his hand in his pocket and took out a flat case which he had carried all the way from Paris, "here's the clasp. But, as I was saying, 'The Jewel' is going to make history in the wireless world. You can get London, you can get Berlin, Rome . . . all you've got to do is to turn this little switch on the outside. . . ."

FINDINGS ARE KEEPINGS

FINDINGS ARE KEEPINGS. THAT was a favourite saying of Laurie Whittaker—a slogan of Stinie Whittaker (who had other names), her father.

Laurie and a youthful messenger of the Eastern Telegraph Company arrived simultaneously on the doorstep of 704 Coram Street, Bloomsbury, and their arrival was coincident with the absence, in the little courtyard at the back of the house, of the one domestic servant on duty in that boarding-house. So that, while the electric bell tinkled in the kitchen, the overworked domestic was hanging up dish-cloths in the back yard.

"I'm afraid there's nobody in," said Laurie, flashing a bright smile at the youth, and then saw the cablegram in his hand. "It's for Captain John Harrowby, isn't it?" she asked. "I'll give it to him."

And the boy, who was new to his job, delivered the envelope and accepted her signature in his book, without a very close regard to the regulations of the cable company.

Laurie slipped the envelope in her bag and pressed the bell again. This time the servant heard the signal and came, wiping her hands on her apron, to open the door.

"No, miss, Captain Harrowby's out," she said, recognising the visitor, and giving her the deference and respect which were due to one who lived in the grandest house in Bedford Square. "He's gone up to the City. Will you step in and wait, miss?"

If Laurie felt annoyed, she did not advertise the fact. She gave her sweetest smile to the servant, nodded pleasantly to the pretty girl who came up the steps as she went down, and, re-entering her limousine, was driven away.

"Who is the lady, Matilda?" asked the newcomer.

"Her?" said the girl-of-all-work. "That's Miss Whittaker—a friend of Mr. Harrowby's. Surely he's told you about her, Miss Bancroft?"

Elsie Bancroft laughed.

"Mr. Harrowby and I are not on such terms that he discusses his friends with me, Matilda," she said, and mounted to her tiny room on the top floor, to turn over again more vital and pressing problems than Captain Harrowby's friendship.

She was a stenographer in a lawyer's office, and if her stipend was not generous it was fair, and might have been sufficient if she were not the mother of a family—in a figurative sense. There was a small brother at school in Broadstairs, and a smaller sister at a preparatory school at Ramsgate, and the money which had been left by their father barely covered the fees of one.

Two letters were propped on her mantelpiece, and she recognised their character with a quaking heart. She stood for a long time surveying them with big, grave eyes before, with a sigh, she took them down and listlessly tore them open. She skimmed the contents with a little grimace, and, lifting her typewriter from the floor, put it on to the table, unlocked a drawer and, taking out a wad of paper written in a crabbed handwriting, began to type. She had got away from the office early to finish the spare time work which often helped to pay the rent.

She had been typing a quarter of an hour when there was a gentle tap at the door, and, in answer to her invitation, a man came a few inches into the room; a slim, brown-faced man of thirty, good-looking, with that far-away expression in his eyes which comes to men who have passed their lives in wide spaces.

"How are you getting on?" he asked, almost apologetically.

"I've done about ten pages since last night," she said. "I'm rather slow, but—" she made a little grimace.

"My handwriting is dreadful, isn't it?" he said, almost humbly.

"It is rather," she answered, and they both laughed. "I wish I could do it faster," she said. "It is as interesting as a novel."

He scratched his chin.

"I suppose it is, in a way," he said cautiously, and then, with sudden embarrassment, "But it's perfectly true."

"Of course it's true," she scoffed. "Nobody could read this report and think it wasn't true! What are you going to do with the manuscript when you have finished it?"

He looked round the room aimlessly before his eyes returned to the pretty face that showed above the machine.

"I don't know," he said vaguely. "It might go into a magazine. I've written it out for my own satisfaction, and because it makes what seems a stupid folly look intelligent and excusable. Besides which, I am hoping to sell the property, and this account may induce some foolish person to buy a parcel of swamp and jungle—though I'd feel as though I were swindling a buyer!"

She had pushed the typewritten sheets towards him, and he picked up the first and read:

"A Report on the Alluvial Goldfields of Quimbo,"

and, reading it, he sighed.

"Yes, the gold is there all right," he said mournfully, "though I've never been able to find it. I've got a concession of a hundred square miles—it's worth less than a hundred shillings! There isn't a railway within five hundred miles; the roads are impossible; and even if there was gold there, I don't know that I should be able to get it away. Anyway, no gold has been found. I have a partner still pottering away out there; I shall probably have his death on my conscience sooner or later."

"Are you going back to Africa?" she asked curiously.

He shook his head.

"I don't think so"—he hesitated—"my—my friends think I should settle down in England. I've made a little money by trading. Possibly I'll buy a farm and raise ducks."

She laughed softly.

"You won't be able to write a story about that," she said, and then, remembering: "Did the maid tell you that Miss Whittaker had called?"

She saw him start and the colour deepen in the tanned face.

"Oh, did she?" he asked awkwardly. "Really? No, the girl told me nothing." And in another minute he was running down the stairs. She did not know whether to be angry or amused at this sudden termination of their talk.

Captain Harrowby had been an inmate of the boarding-house for three weeks, and she had gladly accepted the offer that came through her landlady to type what she thought was the story he had written. The "story" proved to be no more, at first glance, than a prosaic report upon an African property of his, which, he told her, he was trying to sell.

Who was Miss Whittaker? She frowned as she asked herself the question, though she had no reason for personal interest in the smiling girl she had met at the door. She decided that she did not like this smart young lady, with her shingled hair and her ready smile. She knew that Captain Harrowby spent a great deal of his time at the Whittakers' house, but she had no idea that there was anything remarkable in that, until the next day, when she was taking her lunch at the office, she asked old Kilby, who knew the secret history of London better than most process-servers.

"Whittaker?" the old man chuckled. "Oh, I know Stinie Whittaker all right! He runs a gambling hall in Bloomsbury somewhere. He was convicted about ten years ago for the same offence. I served a couple of writs on him years and years ago. He's more prosperous now."

"But surely Miss Whittaker doesn't know?" said the shocked girl. "She's—she's the friend of a—a friend of mine."

Old Kilby laughed uproariously.

"Laurie? Why, Laurie's brought more men to the old man's table than anybody else! Know? Sure she does! Why, she spends all summer going voyages in order to pick up likely birds for Stinie to kill!"

The news filled the girl with uneasiness, though she found it difficult to explain her interest in the lonely man who occupied the room beneath her. Should she warn him? At the mere suggestion she was in a panic. She had quite enough trouble of her own, she told herself (and here she spoke only the truth). And was it likely that a man of his experience would be caught by card-sharps? For six days she turned the matter over in her mind and came to a decision.

On the evening she reached this, John Harrowby dressed himself with great care, took a roll of notes from his locked cash-box, and, after contemplating them thoughtfully, thrust them into his pocket. His situation was a serious one; more serious than he would admit to himself. Laurie had cautioned him against playing for high stakes, but she had not cautioned him against Bobby Salter, the well-dressed young man-about-town, whom he had met first in the Bedford Square drawing-room. Bobby had told him stories of fortunes made and lost at cards, and even initiated him into a "system" which he himself had tested, and had been at his elbow whenever he sat at the table, to urge him to a course of play which had invariably proved disastrous.

John Harrowby was without guile. He no more thought of suspecting the immaculate Bobby than he thought of suspecting Laurie herself. But tonight he would play without the assistance of his mentor, he thought, and drew a deep breath as he patted his pocket and felt the bulge of the notes.

He threw a light coat over his arm, and, turning off the light, stepped out on to the landing, to stare in amazement at a girl who was waiting patiently, her back to the banisters, as she had been waiting for ten minutes.

"I wanted to see you before you went, Captain Harrowby," said Elsie, with a quickly beating heart.

"Anything wrong with the manuscript?" he asked in surprise.

She shook her head.

"No, it isn't that, only—only I'm wondering whether. . . ."

Words failed her for a second.

He was palpably amazed at her agitation, and could find no reason for it.

"Oh Lord!" he said, remembering suddenly. "I haven't paid you!"

"No, no, no, it isn't that." She pushed his hand from his pocket. "Of course it isn't that, Captain Harrowby! It's something—well . . . I know you'll think I'm horribly impertinent, but do you think you ought to play cards for money?" she asked breathlessly.

He stared at her open-mouthed.

"I don't quite know what you mean," he said slowly.

"Haven't you lost . . . a lot of money at Mr. Whittaker's house?" She had to force the words out.

The look in his face changed. From amazement, she saw his eyes narrow, and then, to her unspeakable relief, he smiled.

"I have lost quite a sum," he said gently. "But I don't think you—"

"You don't think that's any business of mine? And neither is it," she said, speaking rapidly. "But I wanted to tell you that Mr. Whittaker . . . is a well-known . . ."

Here she had to stop. She could not say the man was a cheat or a thief; she knew no more than old Kilby had hinted.

"I mean, he has always had . . . play at his house," she faltered. "And you're new to this country, and you don't know people as—as we know them."

This time he laughed.

"You're talking as though you were in the detective service, Miss Bancroft," he said, and then suddenly laid his hand on her shoulder. "I quite understand that you are trying to do me a good turn. In my heart of hearts I believe you're right. But unfortunately I have lost too much to stop now—how you knew that I'd lost anything, I can't guess."

She nodded, and, without another word, turned abruptly away and ran up the stairs to her own room, angry with herself, angry with him, but, more than anything else, astounded at her own action.

No less puzzled and troubled was John Harrowby as he walked into Bedford Square.

Elsie had some work to do; but somehow she could not keep her mind fixed upon her task, and, after spoiling three sheets of paper, gave up the attempt and, sitting back in her chair, let her mind rove at will.

At half-past nine the maid brought her up a cup of tea.

"That Miss Whittaker's just gone, miss," she announced.

Elsie frowned.

"Miss Whittaker? Has she been here?"

"Yes, miss; she come about a quarter of an hour ago and went up to Captain Harrowby's room. That's what puzzles me."

Elsie stared at her open-mouthed.

"Why on earth did she go there?" she demanded.

Matilda shook her head.

"Blest if I can tell, miss. She didn't know that I was watching her. She sent me down to the kitchen to make a cup of tea for her, which was only a dodge of hers, and if I hadn't come back to ask her whether she took sugar, I wouldn't 'a' known she'd been out of the droring-room. I see her coming out of Captain Harrowby's room as I was standing in the hall. You can just see the door through the banisters."

Elsie rose, and went downstairs. Harrowby's door was ajar. She switched on the light. What she expected to find she did not know. There was no sign of disorder. Possibly, she thought, and she found herself sneering, it was a visit of devotion by a love-stricken lady; but there was a cupboard door ajar, and half in and half out the cupboard, a japanned box that was open. She took up the box; it was empty. She put the box back in the cupboard and went thoughtfully out on to the landing.

"I think I'll go and see Captain Harrowby," she said, obeying a sudden impulse, and, a few minutes later, she was walking through the rain to Bedford Square.

She was within a dozen paces of the door of Mr. Whittaker's house when a cab drew up, and she saw Laurie Whittaker alight, pay the cabman and, running up the steps, open the door of the house. Where had she been in the meantime? wondered Elsie. But there was no mystery here. It had begun to rain heavily as Laurie left the house in Coram Street, and she had sheltered in a doorway until a providential taxi came along.

Possibly it was the rain that damped the enthusiasm of the amateur detective; for now, with the Whittaker house only a few paces away, she hesitated. And the longer she waited, the wetter she became. The taximan who had brought Laurie lingered hopefully.

"Taxi, miss?" he asked, and Elsie, feeling a fool, nodded and climbed into the cab, glad to escape for a second from the downpour, and hating herself for her extravagance.

The cab had turned when her hand touched something on the seat. A woman's vanity bag. . . .

"Findings are keepings," according to the proverb, though there is an offence in law which is known as "stealing by finding."

Elsie Bancroft knew little of criminal law, but she was possessed of an inelastic conscience, so that when her hand touched the bag in the darkness, her first impulse was to tap at the window of the taxicab and draw the attention of the driver to her find. And then, for some reason, she checked the impulse. It was a fat bag, and the flap was open. Her ungloved fingers stole absently into its interior, and she knew that she was touching real money in large quantities.

During the war she had worked in a bank, and the feel of banknotes was familiar. Mechanically, she slipped their edge between her nimble fingers. One ... two ... three ... she went on until. ...

"Eighty-four!"

They might be five pound notes—four hundred and twenty pounds. She felt momentarily giddy. Four hundred and twenty pounds! Sufficient to pay the children's school fees—she had had an urgent, if dignified, request from the principal of Tom's boarding school and a no less pointed hint from Joan's—sufficient to settle the problem of the holidays; but. ...

She heaved a deep sigh and looked through the rain-blurred windows. She was painfully near to her destination, and she had to make her decision. It came as a shock to her that any decision had to be made; her course of duty was plain. It was to take the number of the cab, hand the bag to the driver, and report her discovery to the nearest police station.

There was nothing else to be done, no alternative line of action for an honest citizen. ...

The cab stopped with a jerk and, twisting himself in his seat, the driver yanked open the door.

***

Harrowby blinked twice at the retiring rake. A mahogany rake with a well-worn handle, and with an underlip of brass so truly set that even the flimsiest of banknotes could hardly escape its fine bevel. And there were banknotes in plenty on the croupier's side of that rake. They showed ends and corners and ordered edges, notes clean and unclean, but all having a certain interest to Harrowby, because, ten minutes, or maybe ten seconds before, they had been his, and were now the property of the man who wore his evening suit so awkwardly and sucked at a dead cigar.

John Harrowby put his hand in his pocket; as an action it was sheerly mechanical. His pocket, he knew, was a rifled treasury, but he felt he must make sure.

Then came Salter, plump, philosophical and sympathetic. Salter could afford both his sympathy and philosophy; the house gave him a ten per cent. commission on all the easy money he touted, so that even his plumpness was well inside his means.

"Well, how did you do?"

Harrowby's smile was of the slow dawning kind, starting at the corner of his eyes and ending with the expanse of a line of white teeth.

"I lost."

Salter made a noise indicative of his annoyance.

"How much?" he asked anxiously.

He gave the impression that if the loss could be replaced from his pocket, it would be a loss no longer. And Stinie, he of the awkwardly worn dinner-jacket, sometimes minimised a client's losses and based his commission note on his pessimistic estimate.

"About two thousand pounds," said Harrowby.

"Two thousand pounds," said Salter thoughtfully.

He *would* be able to buy the car that he had refused in the afternoon. He felt pleased.

"Tough luck, old man. Try another day."

"Yes," drily.

Harrowby looked across to the table. The bank was still winning. Somebody said, "Banco!" in a sharp, strained voice. There was a pause, a low consultation between the croupier and the banker, and a voice so expressionless and unemotional that Harrowby knew it was the croupier's, said, "I give."

And the bank won again.

Harrowby snuffled as though he found a difficulty in breathing.

He walked slowly down the stairs and paused for a second outside the white-and-gold door of the drawing-room where he knew Laurie would be sitting. A moment's hesitation, then he turned the handle and went in. She was cuddled up in the corner of a big settee, a cigarette between her red lips, a book on her lap. She looked round, and for a second searched his face with her hard, appraising eyes. She was a year or two older than he. . . . He had thought her divine when he came back from Central Africa, where he had spent five bitter years, a trader's half-breed wife and an occasional missionary woman, shrivelled and yellow with heat and fever, the only glimpses he had of womankind.

But now he saw her without the rosy spectacles which he had worn.

"Have you been playing?" she asked coolly.

He nodded.

"And lost?"

He nodded again.

"Really, father is too bad," she drawled. "I wish he wouldn't allow this high play in the house. I hope you're not badly hurt?"

"I've lost everything," he said.

For a second her eyebrows lifted.

"Really?" It was a polite, impersonal interest she showed, no more. "That's too bad."

She swung her feet to the floor, straightened her dress, and threw away her cigarette.

"Then we shall not be seeing a great deal of you in the future, Captain Harrowby?"

"I'm afraid not," he said steadily.

Was this the girl he had known, who had come aboard at Madeira, who had made the five days' voyage from Funchal to Southampton pass in a flash? And now he must go back to scrape the earth, to trek into the impenetrable jungle, seeking the competence which he had thought was his.

"I think you are damnable," he said.

For a second her brows met, then she laughed.

"My dear man, you're a fool," she said calmly. "I certainly invited you to come to the house, but I never asked you to gamble. And really, John, I thought you would take your medicine like a little gentleman."

His heart was thumping painfully. Between the chagrined man whose vanity had been hurt, and the clean anger of one who all his life had detested meanness and trickery, he was in a fair way to making a fool of himself.

"I'm sorry," he said in a low voice, and was walking out of the room when she called him by name.

"I hate to part like this." Her voice was soft, had the old cooing caress in it. "You'll think I'm horrid, John, but really I did my best to persuade you not to play."

He licked his dry lips and said nothing.

"Don't let us part bad friends." She held out her hand, and he took it automatically. "I thought we were going to have such a happy time together," she went on, her pathetic eyes on his. "Can't I lend you some money?"

He shook his head.

"I'm sure the luck would turn if you gave it a chance. Couldn't you sell something?"

The cool audacity of the suggestion took his breath away.

"Sell? What have I to sell?" he demanded harshly. "Souls and bodies are no longer negotiable, even if there was a twentieth-century Mephistopheles waiting round the corner to negotiate the deal!"

She toyed with the fringe of a cushion.

"You could sell your mine," she said, and his laugh sounded loud and discordant in the quietness of that daintily-furnished room.

"That's worth twopence-ha'penny! It is a cemetery—a cemetery of hope and labour. It is the real white man's grave, and I am the white man."

She brought her eyes back to his.

"As you won't borrow money from me, I'll buy it for a thousand pounds."

Again he shook his head.

"No, I'm afraid there's nothing to be done," he said, "except to wish you good-night."

As he turned, she slipped between him and the door.

"I won't let you go like that, John," she said. "Won't you forgive me?"

"I've already forgiven you, if there's anything to forgive," he said.

"Sit down and write me a letter saying you forgive me. I want to have that tangible proof," she pleaded.

He was impatient to be gone, and the foolery of the suggestion grated on him.

"Then I'll write it," she said, sat down at the little escritoire, and scribbled a dozen words. "Now sign that."

He would have gone, but she clutched him by the sleeve.

"Do, please—please!"

He took the pen and scrawled his name, without reading the note, which was half concealed by her hand. Looking through her open fingers, he saw the words "Quimbo Concession."

"What's that?" he said sharply, but she snatched the letter away.

"Give me that paper!" he demanded sternly, reaching out for it, but in another second an automatic pistol had appeared in her hand.

"Go whilst the going's good, Harrowby," she said steadily.

But she had not reckoned on this particular type of man. Suddenly his hand shot out and gripped her wrist, pinning it to the table. In another second he had snatched the letter and flung it into the little fire that blazed on the hearth. He held her at bay till the last scrap of blue paper had turned to black ashes, and then, with a little smile and a nod, he went out of the room into the street and the pelting rain.

He was wet through as he opened the door of No. 704 Coram Street. Matilda, half-way up the stairs, turned with her startling news. He listened and frowned.

"Miss Whittaker been here?" he said incredulously.

"Yes, sir . . . and Miss Bancroft went to tell you all about it. Didn't you see her?"

He shook his head.

What had Laurie Whittaker wanted? he asked himself as he went up the stairs to his room. The girl must have been mistaken.

He took one glance at the open cupboard, and then the truth leapt at him, and, snatching at the box, he put it on the table and threw open the lid. There had been a square sheet of parchment in a broad envelope, and on that parchment was inscribed his title to the Quimbo Concession. It was gone.

He turned with an oath. A girl was standing watching him with grave eyes.

"Is this what you're looking for?" she asked.

Her face was very pale. She held out the envelope and he took it from her hand.

"Where did this come from?" he said, in amazement.

"I stole it," she answered simply; "and I think this is yours."

He took the envelope from her hand with a frown, extracted a cable form and read. It was from his partner.

"Gold found in large quantities near Crocodile Creek. Congratulations."

"How did you get this?" he gasped.

She held out a little French vanity bag, and he recognised it instantly.

"I found it in a cab; Miss Whittaker left it there," she said. "There is also four hundred and twenty pounds which belongs to her."

"Which belongs to us," said John Harrowby firmly. "Findings are keepings in this case, my child. She found me and kept most of my money—I've got fifty pounds left at the bank—and I think we're entitled to this little salvage from the wreck."

And then he kissed her, and it seemed such a natural thing to do that she offered no protest.

THE EAR OF THE SANCTUARY

WHEN MEN, IN ALL sincerity, express their amazement that such a woman should fall in love with such a man, and fall in love to the extent of sacrificing husband and home and all of the big material things of life, the women to whom such amazement is expressed, offer their polite agreement. They will even echo man's astonishment and enlarge upon the incomprehensibility of the proceeding. But in reality they understand. For man to a woman is largely *geist*, certain imponderable qualities which men cannot see in man.

John Hazell had the sympathy of his friends, men and women. Sonia Hazell had the society and violent adoration of Josephus Brahm, a man inclined to stoutness from his youth, a great eater of greasy dishes and notoriously careless about his attire. He wore everlastingly a frock coat with watered-silk lapels and he used scent. The only advantage he possessed over John was a magnificent voice. He sang "Donna e mobile," and proved it.

John was a fine type of gentleman. Handsome in a lean, tanned way, he had grey-blue eyes that smiled at the least provocation. He was clean and wholesome, a rider to hounds, a brilliant Orientalist (he spoke the four Arabics), and an authority on all matters pertaining to Islam. For he had been born in Syria, and did not think in English until he was twelve.

One acquired quality he possessed which served him well in that moment of crisis.

"You can drink, Jack," said his father, the great Scottish archæologist. "You can smoke hemp and gamble and make love to Pashas' sacred wives, and I'll forgive ye. But if I ever catch ye being sorry for yersel', I'll tak' the biggest stick I can find an' ye'll be sair!"

When John Hazell returned from a meeting of a hunt committee and read the note his wife had left, a defiant, illogical letter it was, he sat down to piece together the world this light woman had shattered. He did not see her again until she returned, a broken shrew of a woman, demanding forgiveness as her right, and citing certain acts of neglect on his part which more than justified any failure of hers to keep the letter and the spirit of the law.

She brought back with her a smattering of Polish expletives, a taste for old brandy and cigarettes, and an extensive knowledge of European cities.

John handed her over to the care of her sister, arranged an allowance, and went abroad, never to return. In Constantinople he renewed acquaintance with Sekrit Bey (they had played together as children when the Hazells had a house at the foot of Mount Carmel), and from this renewed acquaintanceship was evolved a new and much-desired bureau.

Josephus Brahm came to Constantinople whilst John was there.

"Hazell Effendi," said Sekrit, a slim seemingly effeminate young man, "though we are as brothers, it would be unpardonable in me to speak of your house. But there is a story about this singing-man which hurts me to hear. That which is behind the curtain is not to be mentioned—*istaghfir Allah!* But if it pleases you, the singer shall sing in hell tonight."

Hazell shook his head and smiled.

"Let him live—only I hear that this man goes to Adrianople to the Governor's house . . . this man has a way with women."

Sekrit tucked his legs farther under his body—they were sitting in the cool of his reception-room, a place of silken *diwans* and plashing fountains, and his even white teeth showed for a fraction of a second.

"A man's house is his citadel," quoth he, and went on to talk of Hazell's strange new mission.

"You leave for Jerusalem tomorrow?" (He used the Arabic designation, "El Kuds," which means "The Sanctuary.") "For years I have been suggesting the appointment of such a man as you. There is trouble—there is always trouble in El Kuds. Sometimes it is trouble over lamps, sometimes over altars. Last week the Copts and the Armenians fought with sticks and knives in the Chapel of the Ascension because the Copts have been granted an extra lamp to burn! You shall be the Ear of El Kuds. Hazell Effendi, you shall have power greater than the *Mutesarrif*, and only less than the *Vali*. Remember that El Kuds is the very centre of world intrigue. There are more political murders planned in the shadow of Mount Olive than in any other city of the world—and we must know. They will fight you, Mussulman and Copt and Russian and Greek, but here we will be strong for you . . ." a long silence and Hazell thought intensely, "as to the Frank singing-man?"

"Leave him to God," said Hazell conventionally.

All this happened in the days before the Great War, when El Kuds held mystery and wonder; before the men in helmets came with their guns and their sanitary inspectors. They have the appearance of permanency—*istaghfir Allah!* God forbid!

The Ear of the Sanctuary? The many consuls shook their heads. There was no such person—he was a legend, a travellers' tale. Hazell Effendi? Neither the Governor nor the Chief of Police knew the name.

Once in the hectic days of war a swaggering Prussian Staff Officer came to the bureau of the Turkish governor.

"There is an Englishman at large in Jerusalem—Hazell, I want him. Where is he?"

The governor stroked his grey beard.

"Effendi, I know of no such man."

The next day the Prussian was recalled to Berlin and sent to the Western Front.

Yet Hazell was alive and his spies covered Jerusalem....

Mostly Yisma Effendi[1] (as they called him) watched the secret men who came and went to Russian monasteries, but most vigilant was he in the detection of miracles. For example:

Once the sisters of the blessed Sanctuary of St. Inokente had found a stone—revealed by vision—beneath which was a key of ancient make (Hadid Ayra, the cunning ironworker by the Damascus Gate, made this, charging ten roubles for his labours), and this key opened an old box which was revealed at the bottom of a well. (Yussef the carpenter of the Jewish Quarter manufactured this for a lira *osmanlizeh*), and in the box which the key opened, in the presence of the whole congregation of Sisters of St. Inokente (on their knees), were three stones darkly coloured and a simple inscription in Latin:

"These Stones Slew Stephen."

Though Latin and Greek strove furiously by vastly circulated pamphlet and authoritative letters, signed and sealed, to demonstrate the absurd unauthenticity of the discovery, yet from Russia and Armenia, from Italy, and even from certain places in Scandinavia, subscriptions had flowed into the coffers of the Sisters of St. Inokente. An idea and an inspiration, and the Monastery of the Ass was not above accepting the lead.

It was the authoritative word of Yisma Effendi that destroyed the miracle. The Ear of the Sanctuary produced Hadid Ayra and Yussef the carpenter. Both had been heavily bribed to keep silence, but Yisma Effendi whipped them

---

1. Literally: "He will hear."

until they spoke. A week after the exposure he tasted a pomegranate at his breakfast . . . and sent for his *tabbackh*.

"Eat this, man," said Yisma, and the cook would have obeyed had not Yisma struck it from his hand.

The pomegranates had been delivered at the door of the servants' quarters. They had not been ordered. Hazell, who preferred pomegranates when they had not been treated with cyanide of potassium, ordered others and made no complaint. In this city of hate where men do murder cheerfully in the name of God such happenings are incidental to life.

Inshallah! It is as God please!

Once he was shot at as he rode by the Jordan. He rode down the shooter and extracted information from him. The next day the would-be assassin was found dead. He gained a strange reputation amongst the followers of Mahomet. They called him a sorcerer, and it was supposed that by a compact with Satan he had the power of making himself invisible, of forecasting events, and of producing rain.

One day he sat in his *mandara* thinking and reading alternately, and his mind was not very far from the Frankish singing-man.

For a story had hummed along his private wire, a story of an errant girl who had fled her house at the word of a man who sang sweetly.

This was no ordinary adventure; for once Joseph Brahm had thrown obstruction into the delicate machinery of statesmanship. Five cipher messages testified to Europe's agitation.

Presently he clapped his hands, and there came to him an Arab youth.

"Mahmud Ali, did you deliver my message to the dragoman of the Nazareen lady?"

"Effendi, it was delivered. The dragoman is William, a great thief and a talker, but he is also frightened. And when I said to him that he must tell the Nazareen lady that you are a magician and can tell the future, he swore he would do this."

Hazell nodded, and with that nod was Mahmud dismissed.

Would she come? And if she came, what should he tell her? Tell her that she was the dupe of a man who duped others . . . his wife? She would dismiss such a warning, and see in it only the spleen of an injured man. Could he tell her that Josephus Brahm was already married, and that if he wed her it would merely be to hold her to ransom? The King of Hellinium would pay heavily for the release of his daughter. The sum had been hinted fearfully on the wire.

Or. . . .

Yisma Effendi might crook his finger, and Brahm would be found with his throat cut in a low house, and every woman in the house would swear to the suicide of a drunk, frenzied man.

That was not the way either. Brahm would die when the hour brought the proper killer.

So he was musing when two people turned into the narrow street and paused before the green door of his garden.

"Lady," said William the dragoman impressively, "this is the fine house of Yisma Effendi. He is fine fellow, ver' great, plenty frien' with *Mutesarrif*—good man, clever magic—I spoke of him."

Her eyes twinkled with laughter, but her lips no more than twitched.

She was an exceedingly pretty girl in her habit of fine white cloth, and the big white topee perched on the back of her head, its green lining an effective frame for her healthy face.

Her mouth was big, the mouth of a giver, but the chin was small and beautifully modelled. Her nose a little *retroussé*, but the eyes large and of a lovely blue. Such hair that showed beneath the helmet was the colour of brown, into which gold had been woven.

She stood before the green door set in the high white wall, the handle of her riding-crop at her lips—she was a little thoughtful and the dragoman formed quite an erroneous view of her hesitation.

Past her moved the ceaseless stream of humanity which all day long, from sunup to sundown, flows through the City of Sanctuary; donkey-boys urging their unwilling charges, long-tuniced Jews, their stiff curls plastered to each side of their faces; slovenly Turkish soldiers; elaborate tourists, Baedeker in hand; monks, sandal-footed and helmeted; Turkish women, heavily veiled peasants from the lands about Bethany—hard-faced, wiry men these; magnificent dragomen, stalking majestically before a sheep-like flock of straggling sightseers. She might abandon her projected visit and, standing with her back to the wall, secure a whole day's amusement from watching the people.

She looked at her tiny watch, then nodded, and William struck hard on the door.

They waited a while and then it opened.

An inquiring old face was thrust round.

"This woman desires to see your master," said William, "therefore, Mahmud Ali, let us enter."

The old man stood back and salaamed to the girl as she passed.

She was in a beautiful little garden filled with European flowers. Rose and heliotrope, great butterfly pansies, flaming gladiolas, and big masses of geraniums set her eyes roving. The white house behind, with the big green jalousies, its domed roof was smothered with wisteria.

Altogether a delightful place, thought the girl, and approved the plashing little fountain in one corner of the garden.

The old man knocked upon the door of the house.

"*Min?*" said a voice, and then, "Enter."

As she crossed the threshold of the *mandara*—this large cool room with its diwans and tiny tables was that indispensable apartment—a man rose and came to meet her.

She took him in with one swift glance from the tarboosh on his head to the red slippers on his feet.

"Oh, Yisma Effendi," said William the dragoman, "this Nazarene has a desire to see you. Before God I would not disturb your honourable peace, but she wished to see this house, being mad and shameless."

He spoke in the Arabic of Syria, feeling tolerably safe.

"Say to her that all my house is hers," said the grave man.

He clapped his hands twice, and a servant in spotless white appeared.

"Bring sherbet," said the young host.

The girl, a curious spectator, was watching him, her eyes scarcely leaving his face.

"Ask the lady if she will be seated," he said.

Before the dragoman could speak, the girl answered in perfect Arabic.

"Oh, Yisma Effendi, let me stand and give me pardon that I disturb you."

William the dragoman gasped a little, and strove hard to remember all that he had said in Arabic to which a young and delicately-nurtured lady, having some influence with the Russian Consul, might take exception.

"Lady," said Hazell, watching her, "all manner of people disturb my rest, seldom so pleasantly."

She nodded at the compliment and looked at the dragoman.

"I will speak to you alone," she said.

Hazell nodded to William, and that man, by no means reluctant to get away to some quiet place where he might prepare needful excuses, went out quickly.

"Here in El Kuds," said she, using the Arabic name for Jerusalem, "they tell many strange stories of you. Some say that you are a magician, others that you can read the future and the hearts of men and women, now"—she hesitated and the colour deepened in her face—"I have come to you because of your wisdom and because I require your help."

He smiled.

"What would you know?" he asked quietly.

"I would know more of somebody who is coming here," she hesitated again, "to see me."

She said this defiantly and with a little touch of hauteur.

"There are certain plans of mine about which I need assurance. Tell me, Yisma Effendi, how will these matters turn out?"

He looked down at her—he was almost a head taller—gravely, almost sadly.

"Lady," he said gently, "who knows the future save God? Yet this will I tell you, that though Ruth forsook all others and clave to the one, she hurt none by so doing. Now it seems to me that you go to shame a very noble house, for I see—" he fixed his eyes dreamily upon one corner of the apartment, and a startled look came into the girl's face, "I see a royal house of three crowns, and a great white palace with broad gardens, and a wilful maid who walks therein and somebody who speaks easy love, being well versed in the art, my lady!"

The girl turned red and white.

"A wilful maid, I tell you," Hazell went on, "who must have her way and disappears from the palace, none knowing whither, and because the man whom she loves is watched night and day—leaves there alone."

He walked slowly up and down the apartment, his head bent, his hands clasped behind him.

"In the Holy Land, men and women come and go and none notice," he said. "Who knows how quickly this lover of yours may come? It is written that wolves will tear down the lamb even in the Sanctuary of God, for wolves are ignoble and beastly. Highness," he said abruptly, "this will mean broken hearts in Hellinium."

The girl was white now, white and shaking. She stared at the man speechbound in her panic, and there was a long and painful silence.

"Tell me," she began at last in a faint voice, but could say no more. From very loyalty she could not put the question. Somehow, in the stilted Arabic they employed, her offence seemed the greater.

"I will tell you of him," said Hazell, "though that is bad talk for a young maid. For there are other women, princess, exalted even as you, and he has sung beautiful songs to them, as beautiful songs as Hafiz of Shiras made amidst his roses, and these he will sing again, but not to you." He frowned again. "I know of one woman—" he began, and then closed his lips tightly.

She walked with knees that trembled to the nearest divan, and sank down suddenly upon the down cushion, white to the lips.

"What do you know?" she asked.

"I know that you are the Princess Helene of Hellinium," said Yisma Effendi, "that your lover is Josephus Brahm in the Frankish language."

She sprang to her feet.

"You knew, you knew all the time!" she stormed. "I will not be intimidated, you are paid by my father!"

"How can that be, lady?" he asked calmly. "I did not bring you here, rather you sought me. I tell you only the things I choose, now go with God."

He raised both his hands as in blessing.

As though watching for this signal, a little boy came pattering across the tessellated floor from one of the draped doorways, and flung wide the big door that led to the gardens without. She stood for a moment on the threshold, then she opened the gold chain bag upon her wrist and took out a tiny handful of Egyptian sovereigns.

"Madam," said Hazell sharply, "I do not seek for gold, but for that which is better."

He waited until the outer gate of the garden had closed, then he crossed the mandara, opened a small door in the wall, and passed through.

He was now in a large room furnished in the modern style as an office. In one corner of the room, under a shade of glass, was a small telegraph instrument. Lifting the shade he placed it carefully on the floor, and with deft hands he manipulated the keys. He received a response almost immediately, and for ten minutes without stopping he rattled the keys with the fingers of an expert.

***

The man who came ashore at Jaffa was certainly handsome in a black and heavy way. He was too stout for the loose-fitting tussau silk suit he wore, and even to mop his brow he should not have taken off his helmet in the shade of the bazaar, for it showed most conspicuously through the curly hair, a certain pinkness of scalp at the back of his head. Yet he was beyond doubt handsome enough, with his bold brown eyes, the careful moustache, the exactly pencilled eyebrows.

Such a man as might easily capture the romantic fancy of a girl of seventeen and hold her in bondage.

He walked quickly from the landing-place and gained the ill-kept streets of the town. Near the centre of the city he found a café and turned in. He was followed a few minutes later by another European, somewhat similarly attired, younger, more sallow, and if his demeanour went for anything, more humbly placed.

"Well?" asked the first man.

He stirred his tall glass of syrup nervously, and his eyes searched the face of the other.

"Everything is well, Josephus," said the sallow man, and he spoke in German, "you slipped them at Alexandria—that I know. There is nothing to fear now, except—"

Josephus Brahm frowned.

"Except—"

The other shrugged his shoulders.

"You know what the minister at Alexandria said—Yisma Effendi."

The other laughed contemptuously.

"Yisma Effendi!" he scoffed. "Always that! At Begradia our friends say—'the Holy Land is your safest objective—but keep from Yisma Effendi!' At Alexandria the same, 'Beware of Yisma Effendi.' Stein!" he thumped the table savagely, "what do I get from this—the girl, yes—but what is a girl!" He shrugged again. "Two hundred thousand *drachma* to restore her, perhaps. Dinoorbeh says the King will pay a million for a divorce, but if he does, how much do I get? Two-fifths! *Sapristi!* Dinoorbeh takes a fifth for the idea, the master of the household a fifth, and a fifth goes to all who helped. This is no coup—as I understand coups. And at the end of it all with success in sight—Yisma Effendi—for heavens' sake, who is he?"

Stein looked thoughtfully out to the sun-washed streets.

"Jerusalem is safe," said he, evading the direct question. "As for Yisma, our friends are very watchful. He has more enemies than thee or I. We could not come at a better time—there is no occasion for nervousness."

Josephus laughed.

"My friend," said he, twirling his fine silky moustache, "nervousness, I do not understand. Somebody once said, 'Beware of—' I forget his name. His wife was Sonia, a dear little soul of whom you have heard. Yet I and that husband were at Constantinople together and he the friend of the great Sekrit Bey—and yet I live! I have penetrated to a harem and lay beneath silken cushions listening to the eunuchs. . . ."

And he told a story to his own discredit. Of a Princess of the Royal House—a veiled daughter of Sultans, scented notes to the sweet singer who had sung in the courtyard of a palace in Adrianople . . . of escapes over high walls.

"The daughter of the great Azrael Pasha," he boasted. "He said he would kill me, yet I have walked through Adrianople since."

"What happened to the girl?" asked the other curiously.

"She was tiresome," was the unsatisfying reply. "Let us talk of Yisma and his enemies."

And for an hour they sat, whilst Stein told of the net which was closing about this officious man.

A week later Yisma Effendi, none called him Hazell, riding briskly near the sown lands, pulled back his horse almost to its haunches, and he did this with his left hand, whilst his right dropped to his riding boot of soft undressed leather.

The four men who had jumped into the road from behind two great boulders, blinked at him and parted their teeth—a ludicrous sight. Not so humorous was the short-barrelled Manlicher carbine which each man carried.

"Oh friends," said Yisma, "what do you seek?"

"*Haj*, we seek the man who is called the Ear of the Sanctuary," said the least pleasant of the men huskily.

"I am that man," said the horseman.

"*Manwitah!*" breathed the leader, but paused before the levelled barrel of the Browning.

"Oh man," said Hazell gently, "you are very near to the mountains of Kaf which border hell—put down your arms quickly."

They had no heart for the business, being only paid men, and they obeyed.

"Tell me now," said Hazell, "who is the man who desires my death, by your head, *Wahiput rasak!*"

The man who answered the function of leader squatted to the earth and spat on the ground.

"Give me, Oh Yisma Effendi, no more than a gold lira *osmanlizeh* and I will tell you."

The horseman shifted his pistol from his right hand to his left. Suddenly a whistling snake of a thong cracked down on the squatting man and he leapt to his feet with a yell.

"Who sent you to kill me, oh thief?" said the horseman calmly.

"Lord—it was a certain Nazarene," sobbed the man. "God knows I wish you no ill, being an honest man ruined by Ashim the Armenian, the usurer of Bethlehem, but they came to me, the Greek—"

So it was the Greek cabal? Hazell had guessed as much.

The men gathered their discarded carbines and handed them to him, butt first.

Brand new every one of them, of Essen make and the ammunition newly issued.

"Go in peace," he said, and watched the assassins out of sight. Then he turned his horse's head and took the uneven road which leads through Jericho to Jerusalem.

At the former village he halted long enough to hand the weapons to the Chief of Police.

"Tewfik Effendi," said the man on the horse, "your district is such that a man cannot ride abroad in safety. Now if this comes to the ears of Nazarene there will be trouble for you."

The stout Tewfik salaamed.

"By my head, Yisma Effendi," he swore, "there has been no theft in this district for the space of four months!"

"There was nearly a murder," said the other grimly. "The governor spoke to me of a new chief of police, thinking because of the dropsy in your legs, you were past the noon. Let there be no more armed robbers hereabouts, on your head, Tewfik Effendi."

"By the grave of my mother," said Tewfik, all shaking, "will you not take coffee with me, Effendi?"

"I sleep in Jerusalem," said the other and went on his way.

He came to the big house near the Jaffa Gate to find a tall old man pacing the mandara. The visitor wore the uniform of a Turkish General, and his short white beard and bushy eyebrows gave him an appearance of ferocity which his known kindliness and benevolence denied.

"Peace on thy house," said Yisma, and drank a long tumblerful of spring water greedily.

"And on you peace," said the visitor. "What did you learn?"

"The man is in the neighbourhood of Jericho. He came by road and has gone the long way round," said Hazell. "To-night the girl goes to meet him."

"A word to the Mutesarrif and she does not leave her house," said the other, but Hazell shook his head.

"That would mean complications," he said. "Diplomacy does not recognise good intentions—there are people who greatly desire the embarrassment of the King of Hellinium. There must be another way of saving her."

He eyed the old man thoughtfully.

"Oh friend of the poor," he said at last, "tell me as between man and man, do you act for your government in this matter—that you command the troops in this *sanjae* I know, but—"

The other threw out his hand with a weary gesture.

"Yisma Effendi," he growled in his gruff deep voice, "I act because you are greater than generals, and I think you set the government moving in this matter. I am responsible for the law and the order of this *sanjae*, and I am told to put myself in your hands. But there is another reason that I move against all stealers of women." He fingered his beard nervously. "It is not seemly that I should speak of happenings behind the curtain, for I am an old-fashioned Mussulman ... but ... before I was sent to this place by my cousin—God give him a thousand years. Ah-min!—I had a daughter ... the lights of my eyes,

Effendi—" he gulped something. "Ai! She is dead, please God, for there came a Frankish man with a voice, to an entertainment I gave to the military governor of Adrianople. And behind the screens the women of my house (forgive me that I speak of such matters) heard … and my daughter … letters and sighings and poems … you understand … and my little bird flew from me," he stopped dead in his walk and turned his eagle face to the other. "I tell you this, that you may know why I act for this Nazarene, I who am a father, and feel—here!" He struck his chest. "Tell me what you call this man who comes."

The nose of Hazell Effendi wrinkled, and there came to him the knowledge that the years had brought a proper ending to the singing-man.

"In the Frankish way," he said softly, "he is called Josephus."

"*Inshallah!*" gasped Azrael Pasha, and went staggering to the wall.

He waved aside the assistance his alarmed host offered.

"Such a man," he asked, "tall—of some breadth—curly of hair like a Levantine Jew, with a tonsure like a priest—?"

Rapidly, fiercely he questioned, point by point, identifying the man, and the Ear of the Sanctuary confirmed each phrase.

"It is written," said Azrael Pasha.

He picked up his long steel-scabbarded sword from a diwan and hitched it to his belt.

"*Leiltak saideh!* May thy night be happy," he said gravely.

"And thine, be happy and blessed," said Hazell as he salaamed the old man out.

—◆—

Azrael Pasha, with eight men of his house, rode out to meet Josephus Brahm in the bright moonlight. He met him riding alone to an appointment by the Gate of Mary—or, as some call it, St. Stephen.

And Josephus was in good heart, for he had a summons from a girl too wilful for regret, too much of a lover for fear.

Azrael Pasha met him in the Valley of Pomegranates, and with his own hands encircled his neck with the silk cord that strangled him.